Look for these exciting titles from

Walter Sorrells

—— First Shot ——

—— THE Silent Room ——

—— Club Dread ——
· HUNTED SERIES ·

—— Fake I.D. ——
· HUNTED SERIES ·

ERratum

Erratum. n. a writer's or publisher's error in publication; *pl.* such errors or a list of them with corrections.

WALTER SORRELLS

DUTTON CHILDREN'S BOOKS

DUTTON CHILDREN'S BOOKS

A division of Penguin Young Readers Group

PUBLISHED BY THE PENGUIN GROUP

Penguin Group (USA) Inc., 375 Hudson Street, New York, New York 10014, U.S.A. · Penguin Group (Canada), 10 Alcorn Avenue, Toronto, Ontario, Canada M4V 3B2 (a division of Pearson Penguin Canada Inc.) · Penguin Books Ltd, 80 Strand, London WC2R 0RL, England · Penguin Ireland, 25 St Stephen's Green, Dublin 2, Ireland (a division of Penguin Books Ltd) · Penguin Group (Australia), 250 Camberwell Road, Camberwell, Victoria 3124, Australia (a division of Pearson Australia Group Pty Ltd) · Penguin Books India Pvt Ltd, 11 Community Centre, Panchsheel Park, New Delhi - 110 017, India · Penguin Group (NZ), 67 Apollo Drive, Rosedale, North Shore 0632, New Zealand (a division of Pearson New Zealand Ltd) · Penguin Books (South Africa) (Pty) Ltd, 24 Sturdee Avenue, Rosebank, Johannesburg 2196, South Africa · Penguin Books Ltd, Registered Offices: 80 Strand, London WC2R 0RL, England

This book is a work of fiction. Names, characters, places, and incidents are either the product of the author's imagination or are used fictitiously, and any resemblance to actual persons, living or dead, business establishments, events, or locales is entirely coincidental.

The publisher does not have any control over and does not assume any responsibility for author or third-party websites or their content.

CIP Data is available

Published in the United States by Dutton Children's Books, a division of Penguin Young Readers Group 345 Hudson Street, New York, New York 10014
www.penguin.com/youngreaders

Designed by Jason Henry

Printed in USA · First Edition
ISBN: 978-0-525-47832-4

1   3   5   7   9   10   2   6   4   2

To Jake Sorrells
Because books are the most powerful
machines in the world.

PROLOGUE

Bob Robbins Jr. and his henchman, Dingle, reached the top of Big Ear Mountain and looked down at the town of Alsberg, Minnesota. In Bob Robbins Jr.'s opinion, calling this a mountain was ridiculous. It was barely a hill. But then this was Minnesota. What did they know about mountains in Minnesota? Zip, that's what.

"We're finally here, Dingle," he said. "Alsberg, Minnesota! After all these years!"

The two men stood silently for a moment, silhouetted against the broad and cloudless blue sky. Around them were broad expanses of empty farmland. Bob Robbins Jr. was the smaller of the two men. He was nice enough looking, neatly dressed, like he was ready to play a few rounds of golf. Dingle, on the other hand, was large and muscular, with a gloomy expression on his weather-beaten face. He was dressed like a mechanic, with his name embroidered on his shirt.

"You smell that, Dingle?" Bob Robbins Jr. sniffed the air. "Destiny. That's the smell of destiny."

Dingle said nothing. Which was normal. Dingle hardly ever said anything.

"Three hundred years," Bob Robbins Jr. said. "Three hundred years of hard work is finally about to pay off. By golly, I feel like a million bucks! I really do!"

Dingle spit on the ground.

"Okay, pal," Bob Robbins Jr. said, "let's go find that girl and get this thing over with."

Then he turned and started walking back down the hill toward a white Ford van that was parked in the weeds off the side of State Highway 9 at the bottom of the hill. Strangely, wherever he and Dingle walked, the grass turned brown and died.

By the time Bob Robbins Jr. reached the van, there was a long brown stripe up the hill, on which nothing was left alive. Not a blade of grass, not a field mouse, not a fly.

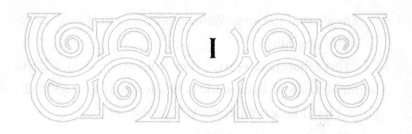

I

There's something different about Jessica."

That's what Jessica Sternhagan's mother always said.

Jessica's mother and father were very normal people. They lived in a very normal town called Alsberg, which was smack in the middle of Minnesota, and they went to a very normal church and they had very normal jobs and they went bowling every Wednesday night and when they talked about stuff at dinner, it was all very normal. They talked about fixing the screen door. They talked about the PTA. They talked about changing the oil in the car. They talked about the new manager at the sausage factory where Jessica's father worked as a shift supervisor.

Sometimes Jessica would look at them and think: *Are these people really my parents?*

Because her mom was right. Jessica *was* different.

For one thing, she had hair that was so blond it was almost white, and she was very thin and very tall. Taller than all the boys in seventh grade. Taller than some of the teachers, even. For another thing, she liked to read. Her mom and dad hardly read anything at all—other than a magazine called *Pork Processing Monthly*, which her dad flipped through every month, looking at the pictures and making faces, like he was trying extremely hard to stay awake.

For another thing, Jessica didn't care about normal stuff. Boys. Grades. Popularity. Beauty. Sports. Celebrities. School dances. All this junk that all the other girls were always *nyip nyip nyip nyip* about? Jessica did not care. She could run faster and jump higher than any other girl in her school. But when Coach Slocum, the girls' basketball coach at the Lars G. Dahlgren Sr. Junior High School, begged her to play on the team, she just said, "No thanks. I find competitive sports uninteresting." Coach Slocum stared at her. He had never heard anybody say such a ridiculous thing. He decided she was emotionally disturbed.

Jessica always knew what she liked and what she didn't. Exactly. She liked mashed potatoes. She liked small reptiles like frogs and snakes. She liked interesting clothing—for instance fur capes, large hats, boots that laced up to the knee, work gloves, very long skirts. She didn't like backpacks, but she did like satchels. She liked going hunting with her father. She disliked small rooms, people with squinty eyes, blue jeans, makeup, people who were full of cow poop. She *hated* airplanes. Hated! Just seeing one crawling across the sky like a giant bug gave her the creeps.

But, particularly, she liked books.

So one Saturday morning when she was walking down Main Street and she saw a bookstore where only the previous day there had been a store that sold Mexican videos and music, she immediately felt impelled to go inside.

A small brass sign next to the door said,

A. Queeg & Son
Rare and Previously Owned Books
PURVEYORS OF MILITARY MAPS, HUNTING BOOKS,

EPHEMERA, ESOTERICA, ETC. ETC. ✦ SINCE 1927

——————— *By appointment only.* ———————

PLEASE DO NOT RING BELL. WE WILL NOT ANSWER.

Jessica might ordinarily have been put off by this sort of message. But not today. Today she had the strongest feeling—like her head might explode if she didn't go inside. So she pressed the brass button next to the sign.

Inside the shop a deep ominous bell sounded. No one answered the door. So she pushed the door open and walked in anyway. The room looked like it was very old, with old dusty books on old dusty shelves. The lighting was poor. A fluorescent bulb in the back gave off a loud hum and flicked on and off in a very irritating way. Each time the light went off and on, it made a sound like a cracking walnut.

Behind the counter was a large, fat woman. In every respect she seemed entirely normal. She wore a flowered dress like you'd find in the very back of the Wal-Mart ladies department, and cheap reading glasses hung around her neck on a chain. The only thing strange about her were her eyes, which seemed to flicker, as though they were lit from inside by a candle, leaving shadows that moved around on the insides of her eyeballs. But, Jessica thought, that was undoubtedly just because of the terrible fluorescent light.

The woman looked up at Jessica, then looked down at her computer and typed something.

"May I look around?"

"We don't sell to the general public, dear," the woman said without looking up. "Or to children."

"What happened to the Mexican video store that used to be here?" Jessica said.

"Dear, I don't have the faintest inkling what you're talking about. We've been here since 1927."

"Hm!" Jessica said. There was a time when she would have said a bad word that, strictly speaking, means cow poop—but that, in reality, means "I think you're either feeding me a lie or you don't have any idea what you're talking about." But after spending weeks in detention hall for saying this particular word in class every time she thought a teacher was saying something stupid, she had finally decided that saying bad words all the time was not a good idea. So now she just said "Hm!" when what she was really thinking was cow poop. Except, really, the other word.

Jessica had always thought it was interesting that people who would stand there with a straight face while they told you lies, or said things that were insane or ridiculous, suddenly got all offended when you used a tiny little word. When, in reality, being full of lies and stupidity was so much worse for the universe.

"Close the door behind you when you leave, dear," the woman at the counter said.

"Actually, I was wondering if you had a first edition of *An Examination of the Battle of Bluntwick and Its Aftermath* by Colonel Alphonse-Marie du Bruguet. The 1869 edition with the erratum sheet."

The woman still didn't look up. "Military History, fourth shelf from the top, eleventh book from the right. It's priced at four hundred twenty-nine dollars."

"I was just kidding," Jessica said. What seemed strange to Jessica was how she had even known to ask about the book. The whole thing had just popped into her head. Like she was remembering something that had never happened. Not to mention that she had zero interest in military history.

As she was talking, a small, rumpled man came out of a little room in the back of the shop. He had an unlit pipe in his mouth and wore a pencil thin mustache like that actor Clark Gable, the guy that was in that old movie *Gone With the Wind*. "My heavens, Mrs. Rosewood!" he said. "Show some manners. Any young lady who knows about the 1869 edition of du Bruguet is certainly free to browse our shop."

He smiled pleasantly. Like Mrs. Rosewood, his eyes flickered oddly—almost like shadows were being projected against the insides of his eyeballs from somewhere in his head. It was obviously the fluorescent lighting—but still there was something creepy about it.

"I'm Mr. Queeg," the man said, the pipe clenched in his teeth.

He stared curiously at Jessica for a moment.

"Wait!" he said. "By golly, stop the presses! You're the lass, aren't you?" He bent over and fumbled around under the counter. "We've been waiting for you, haven't we?"

Mrs. Rosewood looked up, squinted at Jessica. "Oh, my lands! We surely have. We surely have." They both spoke in this weird, old-fashioned way, like people in some cruddy TV movie about hicks from Minnesota.

Finally Mr. Queeg's head popped up from behind the counter and he said, "Here it is. The book you ordered over the Internet."

Jessica shook her head. "No, I didn't."

Mr. Queeg put a book on the counter. It was wrapped in brown butcher paper and tied with twine. Written in red ink on the butcher's paper was a name.

Jessica Sternhagen

Jessica stared. This whole thing was beginning to seem very, very creepy and weird. But it was intriguing, too. It wasn't normal. And, after all, Jessica was not a big fan of normal.

"You may review it back in our reading room," Mr. Queeg said. "Just to be sure that everything's jake."

"Okay," she said. She walked back through a doorway and into a small reading room. A bison head and a stuffed mallard duck hung on the wood-paneled walls, and several pieces of old red leather furniture were scattered around the room. Some framed maps hung on the wall. She glanced at one. It said on the legend that it illustrated the Battle of Bluntwick. Strange, she thought. Same as that book I'd asked about.

"Might I offer you a knife to open it with?" Mr. Queeg said.

"Oh. Yeah, thanks."

He handed her a long curious knife with a curved yellow-white handle that looked like the tooth of a wild boar. The blade, too, was wickedly curved and had a strange undulating pattern that seemed to be part of the steel itself.

She cut off the twine, then carefully slit the butcher paper. The knife was extremely sharp. She was about to set it on the small table next to her chair when Mr. Queeg said: "If I could trouble you to return the knife . . ."

She handed it back to him and he disappeared.

The book in her hand looked quite old. It was bound in worn, cracked leather with the title embossed into the cover with gold letters: HER LIF.

Her lif? Maybe it meant "her *life*." Or was it "her *lie*"?
She flipped the book open.

---

*T*here's something different about Jessica."
That's what Jessica Sternhagen's mother always said.
Jessica's mother and father were very normal people.
They lived in a very normal town called Alsberg, which was
smack in the middle of Minnesota, and they went to a very
normal church and they had very normal jobs and they went
bowling every Wednesday night and when they talked about
stuff at dinner, it was all very normal.

In fact, it started out with the exact same words that
this book did. But from there it was all different. It was
621 pages long, with unusually small print. And what the
book did was tell the story of her life. In very, very, very
great detail.

It told about how she was born three months premature
at the Glenn County Hospital and how they had thought
she would die, but didn't. It told about the time she split
her lip on the playground when she was a year and a half. It
told what her first word was *(fan)*. It told about . . .

Well. Everything. There wasn't a single scrap of her life
that had been left out. Not one.

She was feeling very nervous. But at the same time, she

couldn't tear herself away from the book. Where had this come from? This had to be some kind of elaborate joke.

Only . . . who would play a joke like this? Everybody in the town of Alsberg, Minnesota, was so normal that they would never think of a joke like this. Plus—wouldn't it cost a bunch of money? Moving the Mexican video store. Printing up this dumb book. Having some man and woman pretend they worked at a bookstore that . . . Well, it was just impossibly elaborate.

Her best friend, Dale, was the only person who might think of something like that. Dale was the most imaginative kid she had ever met. But his family was like the poorest people in the whole town. No way he could do something like this.

By the time she'd read about fifty pages, she started getting restless. After all, the story of her life was not at all interesting. She had never sailed solo across the Pacific. She had never bow-hunted for Cape Buffalo in Zambia. She had never traveled to the North Pole. She had never been to space. She had never acted in a movie. She had never big-wave-surfed in Samoa. All she'd done was go to the library and check out books about doing stuff like that, wishing she had been born somewhere else. Somewhere interesting.

"Everything all right?" Mr. Queeg said, sticking his head in the door. His eyes flickered even in this room— which was a little dim but was lit with regular lightbulbs.

"As we mentioned on our Web site, the erratum sheet is missing."

"No, it's fine. It's fine. How . . . uh . . . how much is it? I forget."

"You already paid, my dear," he said. "The check for three thousand seven hundred and nineteen dollars just cleared the bank yesterday."

"Oh," Jessica said, blinking. This was getting more ridiculous by the minute. She figured the best thing to do was play along. "Uh. I guess I forgot."

Mr. Queeg continued to stand in the doorway, arms behind his back, almost as though he were holding something, hiding it from her.

"We close at five," he said. "Feel free to stay until then."

He looked at her intently.

"So who's behind the joke?" Jessica said.

He cocked his head to the side. "Joke? I'm sure I don't know what you're talking about."

"Hm!" Jessica said.

"I'll leave you to your reading."

He walked out of the room, the floorboards creaking under his feet.

She started reading again. All A's in fourth grade. Fell down, scraped her knee. Went on the Lutheran church junior choir trip to St. Paul. Went with her mom to Target to buy toilet paper when they ran out last Christmas.

Oh, God, she thought. *This is my life? It's such dull slop.*

She yawned, flipped to the last page, page 621. Sometimes you had to see how a story worked out to know whether it was worth reading all the way through.

. . . heard the squeak of the floorboards in the other room of the bookshop and looked up in faint alarm.

On the other side of the wall—unbeknownst to Jessica—Mr. Queeg stood with his arm upraised. In his hand he held an Arabian dagger, its grip made from the tusk of a Russian boar, its wickedly curved blade hand-forged from intricately patterned Damascus steel. His strange eyes flickered as though full of shadows.

For reasons she could not understand, her heart began to beat in alarm. The boards squeaked again as Mr. Queeg prepared to fulfill his grisly purpose.

"Wait!" she cried.

But it was too late. Mr. Queeg charged through the doorway and plunged the knife into her heart.

She struggled to rise from her chair, but the pain was excruciating. Blood poured from her chest. After a few moments the pain eased and a darkness settled over her.

Mr. Queeg began to drag her lifeless body through the shop, for heaven only knows what terrible purpose.

Dead at twelve, Jessica's lif had been an utter and complete waste.

❈ THE END ❈

Jessica heard a squeak from the floorboards in the other room of the shop and looked up in terror.

"Holy crap!" she said, springing out of the chair and knocking over the end table. It fell with a crash, knocking out the lamp and plunging the little room into darkness.

As she jumped from her seat, she saw the shadow of a man burst into the room—it was Queeg—the weird knife raised in his hand.

"Where'd you go!" he shouted. "Where'd you go, you little wretch, you sneaky little cow!"

She whacked him in the face as hard as she could with the book. As he fell backward with a howl, she stuffed the book into the satchel she always carried over her shoulder, then ran into the other room.

Mrs. Rosewood was standing by the door with a baseball bat in her hand. "Don't you move, little missy!" she yelled. "I'll show you what-for!"

Jessica picked up a plaster statue of Shakespeare off the counter and threw it at Mrs. Rosewood. Mrs. Rosewood dodged the statue with surprising agility and swung the bat, catching the statue in midair. It exploded into smithereens.

Mrs. Rosewood advanced toward Jessica, swinging the bat. The first swing took out the computer, which fell over and burst into flame. Her next blasted a tin can full of pencils off the counter, sending them flying through the air like darts. Several of them impaled themselves in the wall. The fat woman kept swinging, knocking a row of books onto the floor. She trampled on them, moving inexorably toward Jessica.

"How you like them apples, sweetie pie?" Mrs. Rosewood said.

Jessica backed toward the office, throwing everything she could lay her hands on.

"There's no door back there," Mrs. Rosewood said. "You're trapped. It's all over." Her eyes flickered and flashed.

Jessica turned and ran.

11

Dale Patrick McDuffie was the youngest of eight kids. His dad used to work at the sausage factory. But then he'd gotten his right hand stuck in a grinder, and now he was on disability, sitting around the house watching TV and drinking can after can of Old Milwaukee.

The phone rang.

"Get that, how about, Donna," his dad yelled.

"You get it!" his mom yelled.

"With what?" his dad said, holding up his stump.

"Oh, here we go again," his mom said. "Woe is me, I lost my hand, now I can't do nothing. Show a little imagination for once in your pathetic life and use your good hand."

"It's busy holding my beer."

"Yeah, well, I'm busy trying to make a living here." Dale's mom had a new job, typing stuff for doctors at home. If the past was any guide, she would screw up pretty soon and get fired.

The phone kept ringing and ringing.

Dale sighed. They'd argue all day before either one of them got off their butt and answered the phone.

Dale picked up the receiver. "Hello?"

"Is this Dale McDuffie?"

"Possibly."

There was a long pause. "Are you or aren't you?" The man sounded annoyed.

"That depends on whether you're calling to tell me I won a million bucks or not."

The man cleared his throat. "Look, this isn't a joke. This is Mr. Thernstrom down in circulation at the library. I'm calling to let you know that you have an overdue book."

"I'm shocked to hear that." Actually Dale pretty much always had a couple of books that were overdue. He just never could quite get organized enough to get all the books back in time. "Which one is it?"

"Ah, let me check." He could hear computer keys clicking. "It's called *Her Lif.*" There was a pause. "Can that be right? Maybe it's *Her Life.* Must be a typo."

That was weird. He was pretty sure he'd never checked that one out. "I've never heard of that. Who's it by?"

"It says, 'Anonymous.'"

"Anonymous, huh? So, like, it was written by nobody?"

"Something like that." The guy sounded more irritated by the minute.

"Oh!" Dale said. "Well, then! If nobody wrote it, then obviously I never checked it out either."

Another pause. "Do you think you're funny, young man?"

"I'm not really one to judge," Dale said. "But people

often say I'm totally hilarious." Usually right before they punched him in the face.

"Dale, I think you need to come down right away and explain yourself to the director."

"Huh?"

"It's quite a valuable volume. It shouldn't have been loaned out in the first place."

"I'm telling you, seriously, it's a mistake."

"Inquire at the front desk please. Chop-chop, young man. Tell them the director is waiting for you."

The phone went dead in his ear.

"But—"

Dale frowned. This was totally stupid. He'd checked out a lot of weird and goofy junk at the library—for instance, *Kill or Get Killed* by Colonel Rex Applegate, which showed you a whole bunch of cool ways to kill people with your bare hands. But not anything called *Her Lif*. He was sure of that.

Well. Pretty sure. He got overdue notices all the time. He'd hardly ever turned in a book on time in his life. Somehow things like that always got away from him.

He went over and put on his shoes.

"Where're *you* going?" his dad yelled.

"I'm going to Paris to join the French Foreign Legion," Dale said.

His dad stared at him blankly. Zero reaction. Dale wasn't sure what was worse, making a smart remark and getting punched in the face . . . or making a smart remark and having it be totally ignored.

"Okay, actually I'm going to the library."

"The *library*," his dad said, disgusted. "Jeez, what a freak." Then he looked back at the TV, squashed his empty beer can, and belched loudly.

Dale walked out into the snow and slammed the door. This whole misunderstanding about the overdue book was silly. But it was better than sitting around listening to everybody fight. Maybe he'd go check out *Kill or Get Killed* again.

The town of Alsberg, Minnesota, only had one unusual thing about it. The library.

It is reported that in 1907 a private train arrived at the train depot. The train pulled only one car, which was elaborately decorated in black with silver trim. A very small man wearing a large top hat and a long black coat climbed out and walked down the main street of town. He was followed by three much taller men wearing bowler hats and carrying ledgers and notebooks bound in leather. The small man in the top hat walked until he reached the edge of town. Which was not very far.

At the edge of town he stopped and surveyed the land in front of him. It is reported that he never spoke, but that after a moment he lifted a walking stick with a gold handle and pointed at something in front of him. The three men behind him began scribbling furiously in their ledgers and books. The man in the top hat then turned and walked silently but briskly back to the train. After a moment it belched a great deal of smoke and began to drive away.

The small man never came back to the town. But six months later a large number of workmen—who spoke a foreign language that no one in the town could identify—arrived in the town and began to dig an immense hole in the ground. Once the hole was completed, a vast structure began to rise over it. From what the people of Alsberg could make out, the place was extraordinarily complex, with many basements and subbasements. After the steel frame was built, the exterior was clad in beautiful Italian marble, hiding all its secrets from view. Then a swarthy workman with a handlebar mustache climbed a ladder and chiseled THE ALPHONSE B. MARGARINE PUBLIC LIBRARY over the door. When he was done, the front door opened and a man came out and put a small sign on the door that said:

❧OPEN❧

Everyone, of course, knew who Alphonse B. Margarine was. He was the second richest man in America, the sausage king, who owned stockyards and slaughterhouses and sausage factories and immense herds of cattle and a ranch in Wyoming three times the size of Rhode Island. He also owned the sausage factory in Alsberg. Though, as far as anyone knew, he had never actually visited the factory. He was far too important for that.

Within a day, everyone in the town had visited the library. It was immense. It seemed even larger from the inside than if you looked at it from the outside. The shelves were stuffed with books. Books about ironmongery. Books about the history of fencing. Books about strange religions. Books full of art that was not suitable for children. Books of Persian poetry and German philosophy. Novels by Frenchmen whose very names sounded sinister and voluptuous.

No one in the town checked out any books, of course. There were far too many of them to know which ones were decent and which ones were not. So for a year, the library simply stood there, unused. Then a man came from New York and stayed for a week at the Baker Hotel. When asked, he said that he had come to the library to conduct research. The library's collection of Egyptian papyrus manuscripts, he said grandly, was the finest in the world.

After that, the mayor of the town entered the library and checked out a manual on public speaking. The day after that, the minister of the Lutheran church found a book about missionaries in New Guinea. And soon everyone began to take the place for granted and use it like any normal town would use a public library.

Somewhere along the way it was determined that Alsberg was the home of the largest public library in the entire world. And though it was a little strange, people always pointed it out when relatives came into town. "See that?" they'd say. "Mr. Margarine built that library in 1907. Biggest one in the world. Right here in Alsberg. And after it was built, he never even came to see it. Don't that just beat the band?"

Dale walked into the echoing front lobby of the library. The floor was tiled with marble of various colors, some of which spelled out sayings in Latin that no one could read.

He walked across the large floor and walked up to the long counter and slapped the little bell on the counter that said RING FOR ASSISTANCE.

Ting!

After a moment, a man with squinty eyes, thick glasses, and a balding head surrounded by a fringe of longish hair came out from a door on the other side of the counter. He looked dubiously over the counter at Dale. "Yes?"

"I'm here to see the director."

The man peered at him as though he had just farted loudly. "The *director?*" he said finally.

"This guy called me, said I had an overdue book, and I should talk to the director."

The man continued to squint at him through his thick glasses. "What was the name of the book?" he said finally.

"*Her Lif.*"

"What?"

"*Lif.* L–I–F. *Her Lif.* And don't ask me what it means, because I don't know."

The man turned to his computer, pecked on the keys for a very long time. Finally he turned back to Dale and said, "No."

"No what?"

"No such book. Sorry, kid. Doesn't exist. Not in the collection, not in the world. You've imagined the whole thing."

"Okay, so I never got a phone call about some book that I never checked out that was never written by nobody."

"Anybody," the man said. "The correct word is *anybody*."

"No, I said nobody because I meant nobody. *Anybody* can't not write a not-book. Only nobody can not write a not-book."

The squinty man's eyes got even squintier. He was getting that ready-to-punch-you-in-the-face look that Dale seemed to provoke in so many people. "Oh, I see. You're one of those kids who thinks everything is a big fat joke."

Dale sighed. "Look, I was told to see the director."

"The director is a very busy man. Thank you for visiting the library. Have a nice day." The squinty man walked swiftly back through a door behind the counter and disappeared.

Dale thought about leaving. But then he leaned across the counter, turned the computer screen around so he could see what it said.

HER LIF. BY ANONYMOUS.
DO NOT UNDER ANY CIRCUMSTANCES LOAN THIS

VOLUME TO ANYONE. BY ORDER OF THE
DIRECTOR. EXTREMELY VALUABLE!

Then under that was a word blinking in red.

MISSING.

What a liar! The man had just totally lied to him.
"Hey!" Dale yelled. "Hey! Sir?"
But the squinty man didn't come back out.

III

When Jessica reached the back of the office, she stopped. She looked over her shoulder. The fat woman, Mrs. Rosewood, was lumbering toward her, swinging the bat. With each swing, it smacked into the wall, gouging a huge hole. This lady sure didn't seem to mind smashing the crap out of her shop.

"I've got her cornered, Mr. Queeg!" Mrs. Rosewood yelled.

Queeg appeared behind her. His eyes flickered as he held the dagger in the air over his head. "Let me do the honors," he said.

Mrs. Rosewood stopped swinging the bat. "Heavens to Betsy!" Mrs. Rosewood said. "I believe this child has got me plumb riled up."

Mr. Queeg slid past her and began advancing toward Jessica. Jessica looked around frantically for something she could use to defend herself. Her eyes settled on a large paperweight made of a peculiar amber-colored glass. She picked it up, drew back her arm. It was strangely heavy, like it was made of metal not glass.

Mr. Queeg's face tightened. "Don't touch that!" he shouted.

"Or what?" Jessica said. "You'll kill me?"

"Just . . . put it down. Please! It's very valuable."

Jessica pretended like she was going to drop it. "Oops!" she said. "Whoa!"

Mr. Queeg and Mrs. Rosewood stared at her with their strange flickering eyes. "No, no, no, *no!*" Mrs. Rosewood said. "That's not yours."

"Back up!" Jessica said. "Back up or I'll smash it."

Mrs. Rosewood and Mr. Queeg exchanged glances. They seemed terrified.

"Now!" Jessica said.

Mrs. Rosewood stepped forward. Jessica lifted her arm, as though to throw the glass paperweight at the floor.

"Very well, very well," Mr. Queeg said. "You have us at a disadvantage."

"Back up," Jessica said.

Mr. Queeg took a step back.

"You too!"

Mrs. Rosewood stepped back.

"Keep going."

The pair began slowly easing backward. Jessica began to follow.

Behind them a bell tinkled, as though someone had just entered the shop. "Hello?" a voice said. "Hello?"

Mr. Queeg lowered the knife, hid it behind his back. "One moment," he called pleasantly. Then under his breath he said, "Would you be a dear and handle that, Mrs. Rose-wood."

Mrs. Rosewood set the baseball bat gently against the wall and retreated toward the front of the shop.

Mr. Queeg turned briefly, watching Mrs. Rosewood go.

Jessica, attempting to take advantage of his momentary distraction, darted forward. But she was too late. He heard her footsteps and whirled, lifting the knife. She whacked him with her book satchel. The knife spun out of Mr. Queeg's hand.

Jessica pushed past him and ran full tilt down the aisle toward the front of the shop.

A thin man wearing very old-fashioned clothes was taking off his top hat as he walked up to the counter. "Good morning," he said to Mrs. Rosewood. "I wonder if you have a first edition of—"

Jessica didn't stick around to find out what the oddly dressed man wanted. She plunged past him, out the door, and into the street.

She pounded down the sidewalk in the direction of the police station. As she ran, the paperweight slipped from her hand and smashed on the pavement. Fragments of amber-colored glass flew everywhere. She looked back to see if Mr. Queeg was still following her. And if so, how he reacted to seeing the paperweight get smashed.

But there was no Mr. Queeg in the street behind her.

In fact, to her shock, where the brass sign for the store had been was a blank wall. Where the bookstore had been, there was only a long glass window full of posters advertising Mexican music and movies with Spanish names.

It was as though A. Queeg & Son, Rare and Previously Owned Books . . . had never existed!

Jessica stared. Had it been some kind of weird dream or something?

She turned and began walking home in a daze. The whole thing was crazy, impossible. She kept walking, and her mind kept playing the whole thing over and over. It *seemed* so real!

Then she thought: *what about the book?*

She unbuckled her satchel, reached inside. In the bottom, right next to her math book, lay a worn leather volume: *Her Lif.*

She pulled the book out, flipped to the final page. There it was, the whole story about how she was killed by Mr. Queeg, concluding with the line about how her life had been a total waste.

Then she noticed a piece of paper sticking out from between two pages in the middle of the book. Had that been there before?

She pulled out the piece of paper. It said:

❧ *Erratum* ❧

**Page 621, beginning ". . . heard the boards squeak . . ."
was incorrectly printed. The correct text should read . . .**

And then there it was, a complete description of her fight with Mrs. Rosewood and Mr. Queeg. At the end of the slip of paper, it said, "The Publisher deeply apologizes for this mistake."

She closed the book, feeling completely disoriented. This was *so* weird. She stuffed the book into the satchel she was carrying. She was so focused on the book that she didn't even see the attacker until it was too late.

As she looked up a small figure sprang out from behind the blue mailbox by the street. "Hiiiii-yaahhhh!" he yelled, dropping into a crouch. One hand was held out, guarding his body. In his other hand, tucked close to his belly, was a shiny knife. Her heart jumped into her throat.

Part of her was thinking, *Will this never end?* And the other part of her brain was simply reacting. In one smooth move, she punched him in the face. Her attacker fell down on the ground.

"Ow!" he said, rolling over and staring up at her. What she thought was a knife fell out of his hand. It was actually a fat silver ruler that said PORKMASTER HOG SCALES INC.— "WE MEASURE UP" on it. "Why'd you do *that*, Jess?"

Her heart slowed. It was Dale.

"You jerk!" she said. "You've been reading that stupid *Kill or Get Killed* thing again, haven't you? You scared the kerfoodle out of me!"

"Man, you're a little jumpy today," Dale said. He got up slowly, holding his nose.

"You would be, too, if—"

Dale took his hand away from his nose, seeming relieved not to see blood. "I'll tell you," he said, interrupting her, "the weirdest thing just happened to me."

Before Dale could explain the weird thing, though, Jessica had yet another scare. Over his shoulder Jessica saw an old pickup truck driving slowly down the road toward them. And inside the pickup truck sat Mrs. Rosewood and Mr. Queeg. She prepared to run.

But then she saw that Mrs. Rosewood and Mr. Queeg weren't looking at her. They were just staring dully out the windshield of the truck. They didn't seem to notice her at all. Something had changed about them, something very subtle. They just looked like some hick farmer and his hick wife driving back to the farm after buying some junk at the store. And their eyes had changed. The flickering shadows were gone.

"You okay?" Dale said. "You look a little pale."

"I'm *fine*," Jessica said. "You were gonna tell me something?"

Dale didn't speak. He was staring at something. The book she had just taken out of her satchel.

"What?" Jessica said.

Dale frowned. "That. *Her Lif.*"

Jessica didn't say anything. She was a little distracted by Mr. Queeg and Mrs. Rosewood. She kept waiting for them to do something scary . . . but they simply drove slowly by. For a moment Mrs. Rosewood looked out the window, her dull eyes briefly meeting Jessica's. But then they looked away. There was not a sign of recognition or interest.

The old pickup truck continued up the street. Following it was a long black limousine. The longest, blackest, shiniest car that Jessica had ever seen. The kind that had a silver swoopy-looking woman as a hood ornament. A Rolls-Royce.

To Jessica's surprise, the limousine pulled over and came to a stop at the curb next to them. The back window slid down with a soft humming noise. A very thin man wearing a very old-fashioned collar and a very old-fashioned necktie looked out at the two of them.

"Ah!" he said, smiling brightly. "There you are!"

essica looked around to see who the man in the Rolls-Royce was talking to. But there was nobody standing on the sidewalk other than her and Dale. The thin man had to be talking to them. She recognized him then as the man who had walked into the bookshop while she was escaping.

"Jessica, is it?" the man said. "Miss Sternhagen?"

"Yes . . ." she said hesitantly.

"Elwig P. Craven III, Ph.D.," he said. "My card?" The thin man held out his hand, which was gloved in gray suede. Between his index and third fingers was a card.

Jessica took the card, read it.

Elwig P. Craven III, PH.D., FRSE, etc.
Lingual Engineer

"Linga . . . Lingule . . . Lingull . . ." Jessica wasn't sure how to pronounce the word.

"Ling. Gwul." The man pronounced the word slowly.

"Lingual engineer. That means I design machines made out of words."

Dale scratched his head. "That doesn't make sense," he said. "Machines are made out of real stuff."

The man in the limousine cocked his head. "Real stuff?"

"Like gears and crankshafts and duct tape and stuff. Words are just imaginary."

"Ah!" The man smiled brightly. "Obviously you don't know anything about string theory. In twenty-nine dimensional space, steel is imaginary and words are real. I once got hit in the head by the word *octagonal* and had to spend three days in the hospital."

Jessica and Dale looked at each other. It was obvious the man was one of these grown-ups who thought it was hilarious to say dumb things to kids.

"We kinda need to go," Jessica said. It occurred to her that the man might be some weirdo who would yank them into his car and then carry them off somewhere and do gross and disgusting things to them, and then someday there would be a show about them on TV with all this gloopy music and all these people from the town who probably hadn't even known them, saying how sad it was, the terrible thing that had happened to those two precious children, blahdy blahdy blahdy blah. No thanks.

She and Dale started walking quickly up the sidewalk.

The limousine eased away from the curb and began gliding down the road, keeping perfectly even with them.

"Actually," Elwig Craven said, "the reason I tracked you down, Miss Sternhagen, is that I was looking for the very book that you just bought from those creepy murderers in that store."

"What store?" Dale said. "What creepy murderers?"

"I'm sure your friend will tell you all about it," Elwig Craven said. "The important thing is that my employer is prepared to offer you a sum of cold hard cash in the amount of twelve thousand five hundred dollars for the volume you've got."

"What book?" Jessica said, hiding the volume behind her back. So far the book had been nothing but trouble.

"*Her Lif?*" Dale said. "You want to buy *Her Lif?*"

Jessica glared at Dale.

"What!" he said.

"Indeed," Elwig Craven said. "That is exactly the book I'm talking about. The one you were just trying to hide behind your back."

"I'm not selling," Jessica said.

"Fifteen thousand," the man said.

Jessica had a sudden idea. She opened the book to page 621. Now it read something completely different from what had been there when she had read it just minutes ago. She began reading out loud:

Jessica looked at the peculiarly dressed man for a moment then said, "I said, quote, 'I'm not selling. The book says I'm not selling, so I'm not selling. Period. Close quotes.'"

"You're quite sure?" Elwig Craven said. "Fifteen thousand dollars is a lot of cabbage."

Jessica shook her head.

"Well, then," Elwig Craven said. "If that's what the book says, then it must be so." His window slid up with a soft hum and the limousine drove away.

"See?" she said. "I told you."

"Peculiarly dressed?" the man said. "Am I?"

Jessica nodded.

The man looked thoughtful, then shook his head. "No, I distinctly remember, that's not what happens. I'm quite sure that's an erratum."

"A what?"

"An erratum. A printer's mistake. A glitch in the machine."

"Well, this book seems to be full of them."

"Twenty thousand," the man said. "Final offer."

"It's my book," Jessica said. "I'm keeping it."

"You're quite sure?" the man said. "Twenty thousand dollars is a lot of cabbage."

Jessica simply shook her head.

"Well, then," Elwig Craven said. "If that's what the book says, then it must be so." His window slid up with a soft hum and the Rolls-Royce drove away.

Jessica and Dale watched it disappear around the corner of Third Avenue.

"You think that guy was a pervert or something?" Dale said.

"Hard to say," Jessica said. "It's been kind of a bizarro day."

"I know what you mean," he said. They kept walking. "Anyway, where'd you get that book?"

Jessica wrinkled her nose. "That's a long story."

They walked along Main Street and Jessica told about the store and the book and the nasty people with the shadows in their eyes who had tried to kill her. It seemed very strange, because now everything was so totally normal again. Normal people walked along the sidewalk having normal conversations. Normal cars drove by. A normal plane flew over high, high in the clear blue sky. The air smelled normal, with the vaguely stinky meat smell of the sausage factory wafting through the air.

When Jessica finished telling the story of her adventure, Dale said, "Are you sure you're not making that up?"

"Why would I make it up?"

Dale shrugged, smirked at her. "I make stuff up all the time."

"Yeah, but nobody takes you seriously."

"Thanks a lot!" he said.

"Hey, it's true." She put her arm around his shoulder. It was good to see him. Dale could always cheer her up.

Dale laughed. "Yeah, I guess so." He leaned toward her. "Lemme see it."

Jessica reached in her satchel, handed him the book. Dale flipped through it, eventually pausing. "It says here on page six hundred twenty-two that we go to the Map Room at the library."

"Then what?"

"Here. See for yourself."

He held up the book.

Page 622 began like this:

——————◯——————

— *Chapter* CXVIII —

𝒪n which Jessica Sternhagen discovers that she is a **PERSON OF DESTINY**—this humble volume predicts her glorious and magnificent exploits—Dale and Jessica go to the Map Room of the library—shadows—a frightening pursuit—a close shave in the incinerator—they encounter a person of limited intellect as well as the Director of the Library—something **EXTREMELY TERRIBLE** happens—etc. etc. etc. etc. etc.

——————◯——————

Strangely, the book suddenly seemed to have hundreds more pages than it had earlier. Jessica had been holding the book the whole time. She would have known if somebody had suddenly come up and jammed a bunch more pages in the book. But then, by now she was almost used to the notion that things just suddenly happened in the book without anyone even touching it.

"Glorious and magnificent exploits," Dale said, smirking. "Yeah, *right!*"

"I didn't even know there was a Map Room at the library," Jessica said. "I mean, I've been all over the library and I've never seen a Map Room."

"Me neither," Dale said.

They paused for a minute, looked up toward the small hill where the massive library building sat. Jessica had never noticed it before, but there was something slightly ominous looking about the library. Not quite like the castle of some evil queen in a movie . . . but in that general vein. Kind of dark and stony and spooky-looking.

She shivered. "I don't know," she said.

"Come on!" Dale said, grinning. "It'll be cool!"

He turned and started walking.

V

Jessica and Dale had been best friends since first grade. They had been in separate classes that year, so they didn't really meet until one day after school, when Jessica saw a small boy being picked on out on the football field at Margarine Park.

Jessica normally didn't play much with other kids, so it was unusual for her to approach a large group of them. But something about the situation irked her. A large boy—a third grader with floppy hair, who was always pushing kids around on the playground—was shoving the small boy in the chest. "You think I'm funny now, kid?" he said. "You wanna make another joke?"

As Jessica approached the group of kids, the larger boy with the floppy hair pushed the smaller boy down and sat on his chest. "My dad said your dad's a lazy malingerer," the bigger boy was saying, poking his finger repeatedly into the smaller boy's forehead. Jessica didn't know what a *malingerer* was. But it didn't sound nice.

The smaller boy struggled to move, but his arms were pinned to his side. She recognized him as being a kid from

Mrs. Dyer's class, a boy who was always joking around, always smiling. He wasn't smiling now, though.

"You're a liar!" the boy shouted at his tormentor. Tears were running out of both eyes, dripping down into the hair on the side of his head. "And besides, your breath stinks."

"I hear your dad just sits around all day in his room doing nothing," the bigger boy said, smirking.

"He doesn't have a hand," the smaller boy said. "He can't work."

"Maybe he should get a hook," the bigger boy said. He laughed. Then looked around. All the other kids laughed.

"Yeah," another kid said. "Get him a hook!"

"Get him a hook! Get him a hook!" the other kids echoed.

That was when Jessica made the connection. Her father had told her about this guy at the sausage factory whose hand got cut off and ground up in a vat of meat. They'd had to throw out eight thousand pounds of sausage that day.

Normally Jessica just stood by herself, silently watching other kids play. Other than when she was asked a question by the teacher, she had never said a single word in school. But suddenly she felt a strong need to speak.

"Get off him," she said quietly.

The big kid looked up at her, eyes wide in disbelief. "*What* did you say?"

"Get off of him."

The big kid looked around. "Hey, listen, the mute freak actually speaks English."

"That's more than you can say," the little kid underneath him said.

Some of the other kids laughed nervously. The big kid's eyes narrowed, and the other kids stopped laughing. He started slapping the little boy in the face, lightly, not enough to hurt. But hard enough.

"Stop." Jessica stood over the boy with the floppy hair.

"Whatcha gonna do about it?" the larger boy said.

Jessica grabbed the big boy by his floppy hair and dragged him off the smaller boy. She was not as big as he was. But the way she had taken hold of his hair, he couldn't get away from her. He shrieked. She kept dragging him by the hair until she reached the edge of the field.

When she finally let go of him, the big boy lay on the ground, trembling.

She looked down at him and said, "If I ever see you doing something like that again—here or at school—you'll be a lot sorrier than you are now."

The boy scrambled to his feet and ran away. The rest of the boys followed him. All of them except the little boy.

"My name's Dale," he said. "You want to play?"

"Play?" she said. She had always watched the other kids playing and never could quite make sense of what they were doing. Playing had always seemed mysterious to her. "Okay. I guess."

"I was doing fine all by myself, you know," he said. "I was just about to kick his fat butt."

She frowned at him for a minute until finally she realized he was joking. She started laughing. Then Dale started laughing, too.

As they were laughing, suddenly another boy appeared in front of them. She hadn't noticed him there at all. One minute he wasn't there, and then the next he was. Or at least it seemed that way. But then when she looked closer at the boy, she realized that actually he was a very, very small man—not that much larger than Dale—dressed in old-fashioned clothes.

"Boy," Dale said, blinking at the little man, "for a second I thought you were a kid. But you're not, are you?"

The man said nothing. Instead, he held his fist out toward Jessica, palm up. After a moment, he opened his fingers, revealing a very small cellophane wrapper with what appeared to be a tiny folded-up cracker inside.

Jessica picked it up and looked at it carefully. The cracker resembled an ear. "What is it?" she said.

But as soon as she took it, the man turned and walked away.

"Hey!" she called.

But the man just kept walking. At the curb a very long black car stood idling. He climbed in, and the car drove away.

"Weird," Dale said. "I wouldn't eat it if I was you."

"I wasn't planning to," Jessica said.

Later that day, Jessica showed the ear-shaped cracker to her mother and father. "It's not a cracker," her father said. "It's a fortune cookie."

"What's that?" Jessica said.

"It's a cookie that's supposed to tell you about the future. They give them to you at Chinese restaurants."

"Oh," she said.

Her father opened the wrapper.

"It might be poisoned," her mother said.

"Very true," her father said. "In the future, you should never take things from strangers." Then he broke the odd little cookie in half. Inside was a piece of paper. He read it and his eyebrows went up.

He turned it around and showed it to Jessica's mother. She, too, looked surprised. "My gosh," she said. "Isn't that the strangest?"

"What does it say?"

Her father read it out loud, then turned it around so she could see. It said:

Jessica—Your Desteny—Protector

Jessica was already the best reader in her class. She could have made out the sounds of the words without her father's help. But the meanings of the words were still only vague lumps in her mind. "Yeah but . . . what's it *mean?*" she said.

"It isn't spelled right," her mother said.

"Destiny," her father said. "That's like your future. It says that in the future you're going to be someone who— well, I guess, someone who helps people who can't help themselves."

"Fights," her mother said. "Not *helps*. Fights. Somebody who *fights* for people who can't fight for themselves."

"Same thing, pretty much," her father said. Then he tore the little slip of paper up and threw it in the trash. "Anyway, point is, don't take stuff from strangers."

"Yes, Daddy," Jessica said.

But then late that night Jessica woke up, walked downstairs, pulled the tiny pieces of paper out of the trash, and taped them together. When she was finished, she put them in her box—the one where she kept all her special things.

In the following years, every now and then she would have this feeling that she was in the wrong place—living in the wrong town or the wrong family or the wrong house. She couldn't quite put her finger on it. Just that something in her life was out of whack. Something that needed to be fixed. And every time the feeling would come over her, she would go to her special box and take out the little taped-together piece of paper and study it for a clue.

But the piece of paper never changed, never really gave her a clue.

So after a few years she stopped looking at it.

As Jessica and Dale walked into the lobby of the library, a squinty, balding man was sitting at the information desk, reading. *Pork Processing Monthly*, Jessica noticed. Jessica and Dale walked up to the desk and stood there for a while, but the squinty man didn't look up.

"Excuse me, sir," Dale said finally. "We're looking for the Map Room."

The squinty man kept reading *Pork Processing Monthly*. "Subbasement six," he said.

Jessica and Dale looked at each other. They had both spent hours and hours and hours in the library . . . but they had never seen a subbasement. Much less, subbasement six.

"Huh?" Dale said.

"'Huh' is for horses," the man said.

"I thought it was, '*Hey* is for horses,'" Dale said.

The man finally looked up from his copy of *Pork Processing Monthly*, eyed Dale. "Oh, *you* again. What do you want now?"

"Never mind," Dale said. "Let's go find subbasement six."

"I'm sorry," the squinty man said—not looking sorry at all—"but subbasement six is strictly off-limits to children. *Strictly.*"

"Yes, sir," Jessica said glumly.

The man glared at them for a moment, like he was trying to figure out if they were making fun of him or not. "Have a nice day," he said finally.

Dale started walking toward the elevator on the far side of the room. It was an ancient brass cage, with a door that folded like an accordion and pinched your fingers if you weren't careful.

"Where are you going?" Jessica said.

"To subbasement six of course," Dale said.

"But the man said—"

"He's a butt hole," Dale said. "Anyway, your book said we go there. It must be okay, if it's in a book."

He had a point.

They got into the elevator, and Dale pulled the door shut. They looked at the buttons. Sure enough, there were several buttons for the higher floors, then buttons numbered SB1, SB2, SB3, SB4, SB5, and SB6.

"How come we never saw these before?" Dale said.

"We better not go down there," Jessica said. "We might get in trouble."

Dale smirked and punched the button marked SB6.

"Too late," he said, jiggling his eyebrows comically.

The elevator shuddered and shook and made a soft groaning noise. Then it began to sink down into the darkness.

They went down and down into the dark elevator shaft for what seemed a very long time. It got very dark. Jessica could feel her heart beating. "Maybe we should just go back up," she said.

"Chicken," Dale said.

"That's easy for you to say," she said. "Nobody tried to brain you with a baseball bat today. Or stab you in the heart with an Arabian dagger."

Then suddenly the elevator emerged from the darkness into the first subbasement. Because the elevator had no real walls—it was just a cage made of brass bars—they could see all around them. The first subbasement was brightly lit and full of serious-looking people walking briskly around on a carpeted floor. There were computer terminals everywhere, but no books.

Dale frowned. "Weird."

"Yeah."

They had never seen this part of the library at all.

Then the elevator sank into blackness again. The clanking, shuddering elevator continued its journey down. Each subbasement seemed progressively darker, colder, bleaker, emptier. By the time they reached the fourth subbasement, there were no people to be seen at all. Just long, empty, echoing hallways painted a dingy green. The only sign of life was a very large dog, which squatted on the tile directly in front of the elevator. What was a *dog* doing in the library? It watched them with tiny, malignant yellow eyes the entire time that they moved through the floor, eyeing them like they were lunch.

Then they were in the darkness again. Jessica felt her breath coming very fast now.

"I'm scared," she said. "What if something terrible happens?"

Dale didn't say anything. The elevator clanked and buzzed and rattled. It stayed dark for a very long time.

And just about when Jessica was ready to scream, they came out into the light again.

Bing!

The small bell over the elevator door rang, and the elevator came to a stop with a jerk. It was still about three feet off the floor.

Dale pulled the door open.

"Don't you think we ought to let it go all the way down?" Jessica said.

"Nah," Dale said. "It's probably just stuck." He jumped out. Jessica followed him.

In front of them was a large sign with an arrow pointing to the left down a long hallway. They followed the arrow down a hallway to a large wooden door with gold letters on it that said MAP ROOM.

They opened the door and found themselves in a very long room. The floor was marble, and the walls were covered with framed maps. At the far end of the room was a long wooden counter. Between them and the counter was a maze of velvet ropes, the kind they had at the Alsberg 8 Cinema to keep you from sneaking in without paying. The way the ropes were set up—snaking back and forth and back and forth—it was like they were expecting about a million people to line up there. There was not a soul in the room, however.

Jessica started snaking her way through the ropes. It was going to take about five minutes just to get through all the ropes, so Dale just ducked under them. After a minute, Jessica followed. Eventually they reached the counter. A small sign on a pole said TAKE A NUMBER. Next to it was a number dispenser like they had at the meat counter of the grocery store.

A very large woman in a fuzzy pink sweater came out and looked at them. "Next!" she called, looking out at the room as though it were crammed with people waiting for assistance.

Dale and Jessica exchanged glances. Dale shrugged.

"Number, please," the woman said, smiling somewhat impersonally as they approached the counter. She had a very large, heavy-featured face, and a little too much lipstick.

Dale looked around. "Uh. We're, like, the only people here."

"Number, please," the librarian said again.

Jessica walked back to the number dispenser thingy, pulled off a number, handed it to the librarian.

"And!" the librarian said, clapping her hands together. "What may I do for you lovely young people? You'll be needing a map then? Where are you going? Algiers? New Guinea? Rangoon? Bluntwick?"

"Actually, we were hoping you could tell us about this book," Jessica said. She slid the book across the counter.

"*Her Lif*," the librarian said, pulling on a pair of reading glasses from a chain around her neck. "Well, I'll tell you one thing about it. *Lif* is not a word."

"We kinda knew that already," Dale said.

"Yeah, we were hoping you could tell us a little more about it," Jessica added. "It says in the book we're supposed to come here."

The librarian smiled. "This is the Map Room. If you

wanted me to identify a map, I'm sure I'd be a great deal more helpful. What's the book about?"

"Well, it keeps changing," Jessica said.

The librarian raised one eyebrow. "One of *those* kind of books, hm?"

"Yes."

The librarian took off her glasses and peered closely at Jessica. Suddenly she said, "Oh my! You don't know about any of this do you?"

"Any of what?"

The librarian motioned around her. "*This.*"

Jessica shrugged. "I guess not."

"String theory? N dimensional space? Word machines? Hm? None of this is ringing a bell at all?"

Jessica and Dale stared dumbly at her.

"Oh my!" She frowned. "And . . . how did you get your hands on this book?"

"I went into a store. They said it was for me. It was wrapped in a package with my name on it. Then they tried to kill me."

"*Who* did?" The librarian seemed outraged.

"These people in the store. They had these shadows flickering around in their eyes."

The librarian's face suddenly went pale. "Wait a minute. You're . . . *her*?"

"I'm who?"

"Jessica Sternhagen. You're Jessica *Sternhagen!*"

"How did you know?"

"Well . . . *everyone* remembers what you're going to do."

Dale and Jessica looked at each other.

"You can't remember something that you're *going* to do," Dale said. "You can only remember what you've already done."

"That," said the librarian, "is what is known as semantics."

"Se-*what*-tics?" Dale said.

"Semantics. It means the study of trivial, insignificant, quibbly little differences between words. It's quite an important field of study."

"Yeah but—"

The librarian said, "Well, I must say I'm surprised you're asking me these questions. You must have read the book by now, Jessica."

"Well. Some of it."

"Then you must know that you'll never have a chance to fulfill your destiny if you don't make a break for it right now."

"If I don't . . . *what*?"

"Hurry!" the librarian said. "Before they get you!"

"Before *who* get me?"

The librarian swallowed, pointed.

Jessica and Dale turned to see where the librarian was pointing. To her shock, Jessica saw that the room was now full of people. Lined up silently behind the maze of velvet ropes were hundreds—maybe even thousands—of people. It looked like practically everybody in the city of Alsberg. They all looked like normal people. Except for their eyes, which stared unblinkingly at her . . . and which were full of strange flickering shadows. And they all carried something in their hands—a stick or a fork or a knife or a jagged piece of glass. Anything that could be used as a weapon.

"Run!" the librarian whispered. "As long as you're on this side of the rope, they can't get you. But once you're outside, only the director can help you."

"Where's the director?"

The librarian hurriedly picked up a small, folded map from a stack on the counter. She flipped it open, made a red X with a pen, then thrust it into her hand. "Follow the map! Run down the side of the room. You'll be safe, as long as you're on this side of the rope."

"And after that?"

"Just . . . *run!*" the woman hissed.

Jessica couldn't move. Her breath seemed to be stuck in her chest.

"Hey there, Jess," the man at the front of the line said cheerfully. "By cracky, it's swell to see you!" It was Mr. Peters, her homeroom teacher. She was pretty sure Mr. Peters had never used the phrase *by cracky* in his whole life. But then, in some indefinable way, it was clear this wasn't Mr. Peters at all. He held up his ticket with a number on it. In his other hand he carried a large butcher knife. "I believe

I'm next?" the shadow-eyed version of Mr. Peters said, smiling brightly. "Number forty-seven? Really would love to get myself a peep at a map of the Battle of Bluntwick."

"Run!" the librarian said.

For a split second, Jessica remembered a conversation she and Dale had had once back in fifth grade. They had been sitting near the jungle gym at recess and something had popped into her head, something that had been bugging her for a while. "Do you ever feel like you're in the wrong place, Dale?" she had said.

"Yeah. Pretty much whenever I get beat up."

"No, seriously. Like, are you ever just sitting someplace and you just have this weird feeling in your stomach? Like when you jump out of a tree and your stomach's all . . . waaaaaaaahhhhhhhh!"

Dale looked at the kids on the playground. He cleared his throat and looked uncomfortable. "Maybe," he said.

"Do you think everybody feels like that sometimes?"

For a minute Dale didn't answer. They watched a bunch of kids on the playground running around and yelling. The other kids were playing this game, Smear the Queer. The game had no rules and no real purpose. When you had the ball, everybody would tackle you. That was the whole game. It seemed completely dumb and pointless—but nobody who was playing seemed to notice. They all looked like they were having a million tons of fun.

"I feel like the world is supposed to be happier," he said finally.

"Nah, that's not what I'm talking about. That's wishing. What I mean is, it's not just like you *wished* things were different. It's like . . . what if everything that we see, everything that seems real—what if it was *not* real?" Jessica had never really said anything like this out loud. She'd thought it. But never quite put it into words. As soon as the actual words came out of her mouth, she felt the tiny hairs on her arms and her neck rising. "What if the stuff that was real was somehow hidden? Like it was behind a curtain. And if you got close enough to the curtain, you could *feel* it. Even though you couldn't see it . . ."

"*That* feeling?" Dale looked nervous or embarrassed now. His voice dropped. "Yeah, I know that feeling. I feel it every single day."

There was a long pause.

"Me too," Jessica said finally. Her voice, too, sounded thin and small in her own ears.

The shrill laughing and yelling of the other kids swirled around them. But the kids on the playground seemed distant and colorless, like Jessica was seeing them on an old, crummy TV.

"What if we're not just weirdos?" Jessica said. "What if there really *is* something different about us?"

Dale didn't answer. Usually you could count on him to make jokes at a time like this. But he just sat there, squeezing his hands between his thighs.

She pointed at the kids. "What if we can see something—*feel* something—that they can't? Something that's more real than all of this?" She waved her hands in a big circle.

Dale shivered. "Can we talk about something else?" he said.

"Someday I'm gonna find out," Jessica whispered. "Someday I'm gonna find out what's behind the curtain."

"But what if . . ." Dale's voice trailed off.

"What if *what*?"

For a minute Dale didn't speak. Then, finally, he said, "What if it's something terrible?"

Jessica had started shivering, too. Shivering like the whole world had gone cold.

And they'd never talked about it again. But she had never forgotten the conversation. And she was pretty sure Dale hadn't either.

That old conversation was running around and around in her head as she looked at all the people in the Map Room, their eyes flickering and full of shadows. Was *this* it? Was *this* what lay behind the curtain?

"Come on!" Dale grabbed her hand and yanked her forward. The room was silent except for their footsteps and a soft rustling sound as everyone in the room turned to watch them.

They burst out of the room and down the corridor until they reached the elevator. A small sign was taped to the accordion door.

"Inconvenience?" Dale said. "It's a little more than that!"

At the far end of the hallway, the door to the Map Room had burst open. People were pouring out into the hallway, charging toward them.

"The map!" Dale shouted desperately. "Where's the map?"

Jessica looked at her hand. It was gone.

"But—"

She looked back down toward the Map Room. There in the middle of the hallway was the map. It had slipped out of her hand. The people with shadows in their eyes were running toward her and Dale, trampling all over the map.

Jessica looked around frantically. On the wall across from the elevator was the large arrow that had pointed them toward the Map Room.

Only now it was pointing the other way, down a thin corridor that terminated in what appeared to be a blank wall. It seemed familiar to her suddenly. Like she remembered it from somewhere. It was impossible, of course, since she'd never been here. But still . . .

"Let's go!" Dale said. He started to pull her toward a larger corridor straight in front of them.

"No," Jessica said, feeling a sudden wave of dread run

through her. She wasn't sure why, but she felt quite certain that going that way was a bad idea. "This way."

This time she grabbed his hand, pulled him.

"No!" he said. "It's a dead end."

But when she started to run, he followed her.

VI

When Elwig Craven III's limousine reached the edge of the town of Alsberg, he asked his driver to stop the car.

"Where at, Mr. C?" the driver said.

Elwig Craven pointed at some woods on the side of the road just ahead and said, "There."

What Jessica and Dale had not noticed was that Elwig Craven was not alone in the back of the limousine. Accompanying him was a very tiny person no larger than an infant. But this person was not a child. In fact, the person was so old and had a face so wrinkled with age that it was impossible to tell if he was a she or she was a he. Whatever the case, the tiny ancient person was huddled in a little heap and wrapped in a dirty quilt, so that if you hadn't been paying attention, you might have mistaken him or her for a creepy little doll hidden beneath a small pile of rags.

"This is it, huh?" the tiny, ancient person said in a very high, childlike voice.

"This is, indeed, it," Elwig Craven said.

Then the car came to a stop. The driver climbed out, walked around the car, and opened Craven's door. The driver was a very large man with a scar across his face and small bowed lips that looked like they should have been attached to a female movie star from the era of silent films.

"Wait here, Floyd," Elwig Craven said to the driver, then he picked the tiny person up off the seat across from him, got out of the car, and walked into the woods, the tiny person cradled in his arms like a baby.

The tiny person looked around the woods with interest. Soon they passed a hand-lettered sign that said:

Absurdly dangerous abandoned rock quarry!!!
DO NOT ENTER!!!!!!!
This means you, you complete moron!!!!!!!!!!!!!!!!!

"Whoever wrote that, they sure like exclamation points," the tiny person said.

Elwig Craven made no comment. Elwig Craven had, in fact, written it himself. And it was true, he did like exclamation points. In fact, he liked all forms of punctuation—though the dash—because of its sinuous versatility—was—surely!!!!!—his favorite. After a minute they broke out of the woods, arriving at the top of a large rock cliff.

Below them was a small lake or pond that had formed at the bottom of the old rock quarry. The water in the lake was oily and dark. A fat, dead crow floated in the middle, black wings splayed out in the disgusting water.

"Ready?" Elwig Craven said.

The tiny old person looked down at the water. "There's no time like the present," he said.

"Strictly speaking," Elwig Craven said, "that is false!!!!!!!!!! String theory—in fact—tells us that there are an infinite number of times which are—in many respects—identical to the present." In his mind, Elwig Craven saw all the dashes and exclamation points in the sentences and savored each one of them. Elwig Craven felt about punctuation the way some people felt about ice cream or chocolate or French wine.

"Oh, shut up, Wiggy," the tiny person said. "Just do it."

"Right, then," Elwig Craven said.

And with that he threw the tiny person off the cliff.

The tiny person fell for what seemed a very long time, spinning and cartwheeling, a look of great concentration on the ancient and tiny face. Finally the tiny person hit the water with a smack. Then he—or was it she?—disappeared beneath the water.

Elwig Craven watched for a moment. For a long time nothing happened.

Then, finally, a single large greasy bubble rose to the surface—where it popped with a sound that reminded Elwig Craven of digesting food.

Elwig Craven counted backward from one hundred to zero, shrugged, then turned and walked back to the car.

"What happened to the old dwarf?" his driver said, opening the door.

"Not a dwarf. A midget," Elwig Craven said. "There's a difference."

"Yeah well, what happened to her?"

"Him."

"*Him* then. What happened to *him?*"

"I don't know, actually," Elwig Craven said. "I imagine that Mr. Margarine is now quite dead."

VII

Jessica and Dale pounded down the hallway as fast as they could. Jessica could feel her satchel slamming against her leg. It was slowing her down. But she couldn't leave it behind. It had the book in it. And instinctively she knew that the book couldn't be left behind.

At the other end of the hallway, the shadow-eyed people raced toward them. Mr. Peters was slashing at the air with his butcher knife. Coach Slocum, the girls' basketball coach at the junior high, carried a piece of jagged metal that looked like it had been torn off a folding ladder. He was swinging and stabbing with it, nearly impaling people all around him. The assistant manager of the YWCA pool—Miss Cartwheel? Miss Cartwright? Miss Cart-something—was clubbing the air with a knotted piece of yellow rope.

"Don't look back!" Dale shouted.

But the closer they got to the end of the hallway, the more frightened Jessica became. It was quite clear they were running smack into a dead end.

"We've got you now, little missy!" Coach Slocum shouted.

"By jiminy, you're in the soup!" Mr. Peters added.

They kept running.

And then, finally, there it was. A blank wall.

Well, not entirely blank actually. Right in the middle of the wall was a small button, sort of like a doorbell. Above the doorbell was a very small sign, which read:

⁀ᴏ ɴᴏ⁀
·UNDER ANY CIRCUMSTANCES·
ᴘʀᴇˢˢ

Jessica remembered something that Elwig Craven had said: "Whatever a sign tells me to do, I make a point to do precisely the opposite."

She pressed the button.

And as the roaring noise began and the hallway turned black and they began to fall into a bone-chilling darkness, Jessica thought: *Now wait a minute! When did Elwig Craven say that thing about doing the opposite of what a sign tells him to do?* She remembered it distinctly. And yet . . . when had he said it? She was quite sure that it hadn't been during their brief conversation on the street. So if it hadn't been then, then when had it—

WHAM!

Before she could recall when Elwig Craven had said the thing about signs, they had hit the bottom of whatever they were falling through.

VIII

Jessica lay stunned in the darkness. Every bone in her body hurt. The air smelled like smoke.

Next to her she heard a soft groan.

"Ow. Crap. That hurt." It was Dale's voice. She felt a flood of relief.

"I don't hear them," Jessica said.

"Man, that was close," Dale said. "Did you see Coach Slocum? He was stabbing the walls and stuff! It was like everybody in the whole town just went nuts."

Jessica sat up slowly. "Where do you think we are?"

Suddenly there was a grating noise, and a small rectangle of light appeared a few feet away. "You're in the incinerator," a voice said. Then a head appeared. It was a man with blunt features, a slack mouth, and a somewhat dull expression on his face. "Might want to shake a leg. Sucker's s'pose to crank up in a couple minutes."

"Uh. Who are you?" Jessica said.

"I'm Olaf. The janitor," the man said. "Better hurry."

They climbed out of the blackness. Jessica found herself

covered with ash. Dale, too, was nearly black with the residue from inside the incinerator.

Olaf closed the heavy iron door that led into the incinerator, frowning with concentration. There was something a little dopey-looking about him. He was a pretty big guy, but he moved slowly and deliberately, like he had to think very hard just to do ordinary things.

"Excuse me," Jessica said. "Do you know where the director is? We need to see him. It's important."

The man flipped some switches in a big box on the side of the incinerator, frowning with concentration. When he was done, he said, "Okay, guys, let's go see the director."

As Olaf shambled across the room, there was a sudden noise from the incinerator—WHUMPFFFFF!—and a bright, fiery light shone out from a crack around the iron door. Though all the way across the room, Jessica felt a blast of heat on her face.

"Well, I guess the freakazoids won't be following us through there, huh?" Dale said, grinning.

"This way," Olaf said, walking through a door and into a stairwell next to the incinerator room. They followed him slowly up the stairs. There were no doors as they ascended, just flight after flight after flight of stairs. Pretty soon Jessica started to get out of breath. Olaf, however, trudged on silently at the same pace, showing no sign of tiring.

"How far *is* it?" Dale gasped.

"All the way to the top," Olaf said.

"Yeah, but how far is that?" Jessica said.

"*All* the way," Olaf said again.

Jessica looked at Dale, who shrugged.

And then, suddenly, they had reached a very large door made of polished wood, with a brass doorknob. Olaf opened the door, motioned them to go inside.

They found themselves in a very large, grand office. The walls were paneled in dark wood. A huge desk sat on a thick Persian rug in the middle of the room. Along one wall stood a glass case, inside of which were several rows of books, each one lying open on a small carved wooden rack. There were hand-lettered medieval volumes, leather-bound mathematical treatises, worm-eaten papyrus scrolls, ancient tomes written in Latin and Greek and Chinese— each book appearing rarer and more valuable than the next. Jessica noticed that in the very center of the display, there was one empty rack, smaller than the others, but made from a wood that was glossier, darker, and more intricately carved.

Behind the desk was a large leather chair, which faced away from Jessica and Dale. The top of a balding head was visible. But nothing else of whoever sat in the chair was visible. A small sign on the desk said:

D. L. PURVIS, D.LIB., •DIRECTOR•

As they walked into the room, Olaf closed the door. Jessica could hear his footsteps as he trudged back down the stairs. After a minute the sound of his footsteps faded and the room was completely silent. Silent, that is, except for the loud ticking of a tall grandfather clock, which stood against one wall of the office.

"Um?" Jessica said finally. "Hello?"

No answer.

"Excuse me?" Dale said.

A hand appeared over the top of the chair, index finger extended, as though the director—presumably this *was* the director—was signaling them that he would be one more minute at whatever he was doing.

The clock continued to tick. Its pendulum swung back and forth.

Tick. Tick. Tick.

It was only after a moment that Jessica noticed the clock was running backward.

"Ah!" a voice said from behind the chair. Then the chair spun swiftly around and a man rose from the chair. "Please! Sit!" he said enthusiastically. "I'm D. L. Purvis, director of this humble establishment."

The director of the library was a small, balding man wearing a tweed jacket and a bow tie.

They sat down in two very comfortable leather chairs across from the desk.

The director's eyes widened as he noticed the ash covering them. "Good grief!" he shouted. "What happened to you?"

"We fell into an incinerator," Dale said.

"Of course you did!" he said. He grinned. "I totally forgot."

"How would you know?" Jessica said. "Did you talk to Olaf?"

The director cocked his head. "Well, duh! I read the book."

"The book?"

"*Her Life*, of course! The book that's in your satchel. I read it back in junior high school. Make a point to read it again every two, three years." He sat back down in his big chair and stared at Jessica for a while. "Fan-freakin'-tastic," he said finally. "I can't believe I'm in the company of the great Jessica Sternhagen."

"Actually, it's called *Her Lif*." Jessica reached into her satchel to pull out her copy of the book and show him his mistake.

"Oh, no, no, not *Lif*. *Life*. The correct title is *Her Life*. *Lif*—that's an erratum. A printer's error. That's what makes your particular volume so valuable. All the other four thousand two hundred and eleven copies of the first edition were printed correctly."

"Oh," Jessica said. She kept fishing around in her satchel, but she couldn't seem to find the book.

"Speaking of which"—he clapped his hands together—"you'd better put it back before it gets damaged."

Jessica frowned, still digging around in the satchel. She had a couple of books from the library, some comics, a bunch of gum wrappers, some schoolbooks, a collection of interesting rocks, a tape dispenser. But . . . where was *Her Lif?* "Put it back where?" she said.

The director sprang out of his chair, pulled a small brass key out of his pocket, and unlocked the glass cabinet where all the rare books were on display. "Here, of course."

Jessica felt a mounting sense of horror as she hunted furiously through the satchel. The book was definitely not there. "Uh . . ." she said finally. "I don't think so."

The director raised one eyebrow. "Pardon?"

She shook her head. "It's not going back in the case."

The director's smile faded. "Look. You are, of course, the great Jessica Sternhagen. We all remember and cherish your great deeds and blah blah blah. But you're still just a kid. And that book's very valuable. Sorry, sweetheart, but it really has to go back in the case."

"No, that's what I'm saying. I can't find it." She turned to Dale. "I didn't give it to you, did I?"

Dale shook his head.

The director's face slowly went white. "But . . . where . . ."

"It must have fallen out in the incinerator."

The director swallowed. Then he picked up his phone, dialed a number. "Olaf!" he shouted. "Turn off the incinerator! Now!"

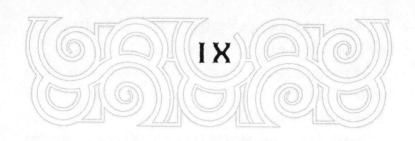

IX

Two minutes later, Jessica, Dale, and the director were watching as Olaf poked a long stick around in the incinerator.

"Don't you have a flashlight or something?" the director said impatiently.

"Wouldn't do no good," the janitor said. "Too fulla smoke to see nothing in there. We gotta wait to know for sure."

And, in fact, a small cloud of smoke had already escaped through the iron door and was slowly filling the room.

"Anyways," Olaf said, "it ain't in there."

"You're *sure*."

Olaf nodded.

"Did it get burned up?" Dale said.

Olaf scratched his face, sighed, shrugged. "Coulda."

The director put his face in his hands. "This is disastrous," he said. "Totally *disastrous!*" Then he started rocking back and forth like some little kid whose mom had forgotten to pick him up from school.

"Why is this such a big deal?" Dale said. "It's just a book."

"Just a *book?*" The director whirled. "Young man, this is her destiny!"

"*What's* my destiny?" Jessica said.

"Didn't you read the book?" The director's eyes widened. "You didn't read the book?"

Jessica cocked her head slightly. "Not . . . you know . . . the whole thing. It was mostly a bunch of boring junk about going to social studies class and stuff."

The director put his hands on her shoulders, looked her in the eye. "Jessica," he said, "the book is very clear about what lies before you."

She shrugged. "Like . . . what?"

"Jessica." His face was so close now that she could smell the tea he'd obviously been drinking. "It's your destiny to save the universe."

Jessica waited a few seconds for the director to start laughing or something. This was obviously all a big practical joke.

Finally Dale burst out in a loud bark of a laugh.

"You find this humorous?" Dr. D. L. Purvis said.

"Come on. You're kidding, right?" Dale said.

The director shook his head slowly. There wasn't even a ghost of humor in his face.

"But if I don't have the book . . ." Jessica said, "how do I know what I'm supposed to do?"

The director hesitated. The smoke, which was slowly filling the room, got so thick that Jessica couldn't see the director at all. Finally his disembodied voice came out of the smoky gloom. "Perhaps I'd better tell you about word machines."

X

"Every book is a machine." Dr. D. L. Purvis had led them back up to his office, and now they were sitting in the big leather chairs again.

"That's what Elwig P. Craven told us," Dale said. "But that's silly."

"You've met Elwig Craven?" The director looked astonished.

Jessica and Dale nodded.

"Oh my! This is getting more peculiar by the moment." He rubbed his face nervously. "Anyway. I was telling you about word machines." He cleared his throat. "All right. In our world, a book is just what it seems to be. Words on a page."

"Wait, wait, wait," Jessica interrupted. "What do you mean by 'our world'?"

"Well, not to get too technical, but the universe has twenty-nine dimensions. Our universe only uses four of them. Length, width, height plus . . ." He waited. "Anyone?"

"Time," Dale said.

"Time. Very good. We can move in three dimensions more or less however we want. But time is like a string, and we just move along it without being able to go forward or backward. At least . . . normally that's how it works. Sometimes we refer to our universe as 'Four World.' But as it happens, there are other universes, just like ours . . . only different. Some use all twenty-nine dimensions, some don't. But they're all connected. Things that happen here affect other universes. And things that happen in other universes affect things here. Books are little machines that communicate between our universe and other universes."

"How do we know this?"

"Elwig Craven worked out all the mathematics. It's way beyond my ability to comprehend. But it turns out that our universe has a unique role in the greater universe of twenty-nine dimensions. It's a sort of balance point. Like the middle of a teeter-totter. If the balance point shifts, everything can get out of whack. Word machines are used to maintain that balance."

"How?"

"This is a bit of an oversimplification, you understand—but imagine that there is a dark part of the universe and a light part of the universe. We could imagine that the dark part is destructive and evil, while the light part is creative and good. But again, that's an oversimplification. The dark part is always trying to absorb and destroy the light part. Apparently books can create light, repair holes, fix darkness. Of course, they can be used to do just the opposite, too."

"But how does it *work*?" Jessica was feeling frustrated.

The director shrugged. "No one knows exactly. All that we know is that good books are more powerful than bad books."

"How do you define a good book?" Dale said.

"Well, it has an exciting event at the beginning. Then someone's in trouble. Someone that you'd like if you met them. They try to get themselves out of trouble. Obstacles arise. The closer they get to getting out of trouble, the worse the trouble seems to get. Then in the end, everything works out. That's how it's done."

"But that's . . ." Jessica wrinkled her nose. "But that's dumb. That's just a story."

"Yeah," Dale said. "Besides, if it's such a big deal, why don't people just sit around writing books like that all the time. We could just all write books and fix everything, and then there wouldn't be anything wrong in the universe."

"Ah!" The director smiled. "Now I see where you're going. You're saying it sounds easy."

"Well, the way you put it, yeah."

"It does, doesn't it? And, in fact, every moron in the world thinks they can write a good book. But it's harder than it looks, believe me."

"How do you know?"

"I've tried. I've written five novels so far. And they're

all wretched. Wretched, miserable, stinking failures." For a moment the director looked sad and bitter. Then he smiled thinly. "But . . . that's neither here nor there, is it?" Dr. D. L. Purvis pointed at Jessica. "And then, occasionally, there are special books. Like the one about you."

"*Her Lif.*"

"Exactly. We don't know who wrote *Her Life*. Or why. All we know is that there's something unusual about it. You see, every time a person makes a decision, it affects the universe. If I decide to wear a red shirt today instead of a blue shirt, it affects things. Maybe a lot, maybe a little. But there are people whose choices have very strong effects on the universe. Jessica, you're one of those people. And here's what that book seems to do. It seems to make it so that when you make a choice, that choice affects not only the future . . . but also the past."

Jessica felt a quivery sensation in her stomach. This whole thing seemed impossible. How could you affect the past by something you did today. It just didn't compute. "But that's not possible!"

"It is. Here's how it works." The director looked thoughtfully at the ceiling. "Okay. Imagine that you're walking down a path. After you've been walking awhile, the path splits in two. One path has a sign that says THIS WAY TO ICE CREAM, and the other path says THIS WAY TO CAKE. Now, you like cake, but you also like ice cream. So you have to make a decision. Cake or ice cream?"

"Cake," Dale said. "Definitely."

"Ice cream," Jessica said. "I mean . . . unless it was carrot cake. Carrot cake—that would be a toss-up. If it was carrot cake, I think I'd try to run really fast. Then I could go both ways."

"Both ways." Director Purvis laughed. "Interesting you should put it that way. Suppose the universe split in two at the moment you made the choice. And instead of one person making one choice, you had two universes. And two yous. Does that make sense?"

"Other than the fact that it's totally dumb and impossible, you mean?" Dale said.

"In one universe," the library director continued, ignoring him, "Jessica Number One heads off and gets the carrot cake. In the other universe, Jessica Number Two goes the other way and gets the ice cream."

"We all know it doesn't work like that," Dale said.

The library director cocked his head. "Do we?"

"Oh, come on!" Dale said.

"I am told," the library director said, "that, in fact, it does work like that. Because, of course, Jessica Number One and Jessica Number Two never meet."

"Says who?" Jessica said.

"Elwig Craven, for one."

Jessica and Dale looked at each other skeptically.

"Here's how Dr. Craven explained it to me," the director said. "Imagine that the universe is a giant road. That road moves through time. It goes on forever in both directions. Now, every time somebody decides something, you get a fork in the road. One universe goes off in one direction, another universe goes off in the other direction. New roads are constantly splitting off. There's a main road . . . but these other roads keep growing. Infinite numbers of them. Sometimes they go off in some wrong direction and they just sort of peter out in the woods and disappear. Or sometimes they just kind of grow back into the main road. That main road, is—so to speak—the true and correct universe."

Jessica felt like she was getting a headache. This was all just too complicated.

"In the long run, the main road is always there. It's sort of the balance point in the system. All these other roads come and go. But if, somehow, the main road were to disappear . . . everything would go out of whack, the universe would veer off in some horrible direction and . . . things would get very bad."

"Okay," Jessica said. "I'm still trying to understand what that has to do with this book."

"The book is a sort of transportation device. When you have it in your hands, it moves you from one universe— one 'road,' if you will—to another. Normally Jessica Number One and Jessica Number Two can never be aware of each other. Cake Jessica will always be Cake Jessica. And Ice Cream Jessica will always be Ice Cream Jessica. But this book, Jessica, it allows you to move—with all your memories of the true and correct universe—from one universe to another. There is a right choice, you see. Let's say cake is the right choice. That book allows you to move from Cake World to Ice Cream World. But you'll still remember Cake World. You'll still remember the way the world is *supposed* to be."

"Jeez." Dale held his temples with his hands. "You're freaking me out here."

"It gets even stranger. See, Jessica, for you to make certain choices, something different may have had to happen in the past. So let's say that the only reason you would choose ice cream instead of cake was if Dale wore a blue shirt instead of a green shirt. The moment you moved from Cake World to Ice Cream World, Dale's shirt would change colors."

"But that's dumb!" Jessica said. "What difference does it make if his shirt changes colors?"

"It just does. I'll give you a real example. Today when you were in the bookstore, Jessica, you dropped a paperweight. Remember?"

"Sure. Those people acted all weird when I grabbed it—like it was magic or something."

"Exactly. And yet, in fact, it wasn't magical. It wasn't a time travel device. It didn't have some kind of force field around it. It was just a cheap piece of glass. But it just so happened that breaking that particular paperweight—while you had the book in your possession—made A. Queeg &

Sons Rare Books unhappen. It ceased to exist. Just like Dale's shirt would change colors if you chose ice cream over cake."

Jessica frowned. "So you're saying *I* changed history? *Me*? A little girl?"

"That's right. You made a sixty-year-old store disappear from the face of the earth. Just by dropping that paperweight."

"Could it be something bigger than that?" Dale said. "Something . . . I don't know, something in history? Like you could go back and change who the first president was or something?"

The director looked at Dale for a long time. "I'm afraid it could be something much bigger than that."

"So . . . in theory, you could do it the other way around?" Dale said.

"What do you mean?"

"Well, like if there was something in the past you wanted to change. Let's say my favorite dog got run over by a car. If Jessica had that book in her hands, there might be something she could do to . . . uh . . . un-run over my dog. Right?"

"That's a very dangerous way of looking at things," the director said sharply.

"Why?"

"Haven't you been listening? Jessica has a role to play! She's a guardian of the true and correct universe!"

"So?"

"Well, she can't go running around changing the whole universe just to save your dog. In the true and correct universe, your dog dies. It's sad, but that's just how it is."

"Why? I'd think that in the true and correct universe everybody would be happy and bad stuff would never happen."

The director smiled sadly. "Wouldn't that be nice? But I'm afraid the universe doesn't work that way."

"Okay, hold up, hold up!" Jessica said. "What's this 'guardian of the universe' thing?"

"That's what I'm trying to tell you. It's your destiny to make sure that nobody yanks the universe out of balance."

"But who would do something like that?"

The director's face went a little pale. "Trust me. There are people out there. Forces. Things." He hesitated. "As a matter of fact, they want to do exactly the sort of thing Dale is talking about. They want to change the course of events. Past, present, future."

"Why?"

"Because they want things they aren't supposed to have."

"Like what?"

"Power, money, fame, all the ice cream they can eat . . . all that sort of thing."

"Who are we talking about here?" Jessica said.

"That's above my pay grade, I'm afraid," the director said. "But I presume that you'll know when you find them."

"But—"

The director stood abruptly and clapped his hands together. "Well, we've been talking for far too long. Jessica, you need to find that book. Someone *is* trying to unbalance the universe. And without that book, you won't be able to stop them."

Jessica blinked. "But—"

"Go." He pointed at the door. "Find the book."

After they got out of the library, Jessica said, "Let's go home and eat. Then meet me back at the library at one-thirty. We'll figure out where the book is when we're not so hungry."

Dale shrugged. "Okay," he said.

When Jessica got home, there was a car she didn't recognize sitting in the driveway. Her mom had been selling Mary Kay cosmetics for a while, though, and sometimes people Jessica didn't know came to the house to get makeovers.

Jessica opened the door and bounded into the house.

Only . . . something very strange had happened. All the furniture was different.

"Mom?" Jessica called.

A woman poked her head around the corner from the kitchen. It was Mrs. Ellis, a friend of her mom's. She looked extremely puzzled. "Jess?" she said.

"Hi, Mrs. Ellis. Is Mom home?"

Mrs. Ellis continued to look extremely confused. "You mean . . . is she *here*?"

Duh, Jessica thought. "Yeah. Is she giving you a make-over or something?"

Mrs. Ellis looked at her blankly.

"Well, tell her I'm in my room," Jessica said, bounding up the stairs.

But by the time she reached the top of the stairs, Jessica had a very odd, sick feeling. Something totally strange was going on. There were family photos hanging on the walls of the staircase. Only, they weren't photos of Jessica and her family. They were photos of the Ellises.

Jessica kept going, though, and pushed open the door to her room. Except that it wasn't her room at all. Lying on his back on the bed was Ben Ellis, Mrs. Ellis's son, who was about five years older than Jessica. His eyes were closed, and he was wearing headphones, loud music blaring out of them. His lips moved as he sang silently to the music. There were posters of bands with long hair and black clothes covering the walls, a radio-controlled car with nubby tires on the floor, a TV on the dresser, which soundlessly played a kung fu movie, Jackie Chan hitting some guy in the face with a ladder.

Jessica backed slowly out of the room, her heart banging in her chest. *Okay, something really bad is happening here.* It was like . . . this wasn't her house anymore.

Mrs. Ellis was following Jessica up the stairs, staring at her nervously.

"Jessica?" Mrs. Ellis said. "Jess?"

Jessica smiled weakly. "Mom's really not here?"

"Jessica? Are you all right?"

"Uh. I'm fine. It's just . . ." She searched for some kind of explanation for why she had just invaded a house that she seemed not to live in anymore. "Uh . . . Mom told me she was coming here today to sell you some Mary Kay stuff."

Mrs. Ellis cocked her head. "Since when has your mother sold Mary Kay?"

Jessica felt something queasy moving in her stomach. "I . . . uh . . ." She cleared her throat. "I'm so sorry. I'm really embarrassed." She pushed past Mrs. Ellis, ran down the stairs.

Mrs. Ellis's husband was standing in the living room with a copy of *Pork Processing Monthly* in his hand. "Hey there, Jess!" he said heartily. "We sure miss your dad down at the factory. How's he holding up?"

"Uh, he's fine," Jessica said.

"Tell him we're thinking about him, huh?" Mr. Ellis said.

"Sure." Jessica couldn't think of anything to do but flee. She ran to the door, opened it . . . then realized she had no idea where she'd go next. "Um, Mr. Ellis?"

"Yeah, hon?"

"Do you know where I live?"

Mr. Ellis blinked.

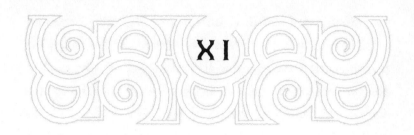

XI

Dale had told Jessica that he was going to go home to eat. But the truth was, he didn't feel like going home.

First thing, Dale didn't really like being at home. There were too many people in the house, all his brothers and sisters and his parents and five or six dogs. And everybody—except for one or two of the dogs, maybe—was in a bad mood. Always. Plus, half the time there was nothing in the house to eat anyway. A loaf of white bread, maybe some peanut butter or some baloney. But that was it.

When Dale was by himself, he liked to slip through the fence behind the sausage factory. The factory had a test kitchen there, where they tested new kinds of sausage. Sometimes when he was hungry, he'd knock on the door and talk to the old security guard, Mr. Naami. Mr. Naami always had a loaf of really good bread, and after they'd talked a little, he'd say, "Here, kid, try this new sausage, see what you think."

And they'd discuss whether the new sausage was any good or not. They'd discuss the spices and the way it felt in your mouth and all kinds of stuff. Mr. Naami had been an inspector in the factory before he retired, and he knew everything there was to know about sausage. He just worked as a security guard, he said, because being retired was boring, sitting around the house all day.

Dale opened the door next to the small sign that read ALPHONSE B. MARGARINE TEST KITCHEN AND LABORATORY, and poked his head inside. To his surprise Mr. Naami wasn't sitting in his usual chair by the door. Instead, sprawled in the chair, was a young woman with large features, wearing a uniform that was about three sizes too tight for her round body. She was chewing furiously on some gum.

"What!" the female security guard said. "How'd you get in here, kid?"

"Ummm . . ." Dale looked over her shoulder to see if Mr. Naami was there. "Where's Mr. Naami?"

The female security guard blew a bubble with her bubble gum. "Who?"

"Mr. Naami. The regular security guard."

"I don't know who you're talking about. Get outta here."

Dale could smell the sausage cooking back there in the test lab. It smelled really good. He could smell chives and basil and pepper. Maybe a little cumin, too? It must be the new Asian Delite sausage that they were working on. The smell made Dale realize he was starving. There hadn't really been anything for breakfast at home that morning. "Sometimes Mr. Naami gives me some sausage. You know . . . to help test the flavor."

"There ain't no Mr. Naami. Get that outta your head. Now, I asked you a question. How did you get in here? It's not allowable for you to be in this facility."

"Not *allowable?*" Dale said. "I'm not sure that's even a word."

The new security guard was smacking away harder and harder on her gum, her eyes narrowing. "Get outta here, you freeloading little smart aleck. Before I call the cops."

Dale couldn't believe how good the sausage smelled. Man! This morning there hadn't been anything at home but peanut butter and bread. Probably his brothers and sisters had eaten that by now.

Dale sighed and retreated out the door. He looked back after a minute and saw the security guard staring at him through the glass. He turned the corner quickly and walked behind the building so she couldn't spy on him anymore. He supposed he ought to go home. But he really didn't want to. As he slouched by the loading dock, a man in a white lab coat came out the back door of the test kitchen and dumped a huge pile of sausages in the trash.

When the man had disappeared again, Dale walked over and looked at the sausage. It was the Asian Delite they'd been testing. Mr. Naami said it was really just Polish sausage with some different spices in it. Polish sausage—Dale's favorite kind. He leaned over and looked at it. It looked just fine. Still steaming from the grill. Sometimes they tested sausage for things other than taste. Consistency, texture, seeing if it fell apart when you cooked it, stuff like that.

Then they just dumped it. He snatched up a piece of Polish sausage and popped it in his mouth. Mm! Yes! Perfect!

He had wolfed down a couple pieces of sausage when suddenly it hit him how depressing this was.

I'm eating food out of the trash, he thought. *The trash!* The truth was, his family was so poor and so pathetic that digging Asian Delite sausage out of the trash just seemed like a reasonable thing to do. That's what it came down to. *I'm poor. I'm poor and miserable.*

Dale grabbed two more pieces of sausage just as the chubby security guard charged out the back door of the building.

"Hey!" she yelled. "Get outta there!"

Dale could see just by the way she wobbled and jiggled as she ran that there was no way she could catch him. He threw one of the sausages at her.

Slap! It caught her square in the middle of the forehead. For a moment the sausage just stuck there, the greasy juice running down her face. "Can I just say, that looks very nice on you?" Dale called.

"I'm gonna *kill* you!" she yelled.

Dale was off like a shot, laughing his head off.

But after he climbed over the fence and disappeared into the woods behind the factory, a feeling of gloom descended over him again.

Dale had a sort of hideout in the woods. A place he'd never even told Jess about. He wasn't sure why he hadn't.

But it had something to do with the fact that Jessica had so many nice things in her life. And he had . . . well . . . pretty much nothing. Other than a smart-alecky sense of humor anyway. So this was his one little private thing, his and his alone.

For years, he'd come here. It was an old car abandoned in the middle of the woods. A black Ford Fairlane, rusted out, no engine, the windows busted out. It was his place to sit and think and be alone.

Dale had almost told Jessica about the place once. It was the day they had the conversation about what if the world wasn't really what it seemed like. That day she had said, "What if the real world was covered up, like it was hidden behind a curtain?" It had all seemed crazy at the time. Crazy and spooky—and he hadn't wanted to talk about it.

He opened the door, sat down, put his head on the steering wheel. There were a lot of things that he'd imagined over the years when he came here—that he was driving a tank in the Battle of the Bulge; that he was steering a Land Rover across the Sahara desert; that he was the emperor of China, being carried in a sedan chair to the Forbidden City . . . All kinds of stuff. But the fantasy he'd had the most was totally different. It had nothing to do with exploring or fighting or exotic adventures.

He called it his "normal life dream."

It was something he'd thought about since he was probably five or six years old. In his fantasy, everybody in the family was happy and they lived in a nice house and nobody argued. His father wore golf shirts and went to work every day and laughed all the time. And Dale's favorite part of the fantasy never changed. It was always the same. He'd be walking home one day, on a beautiful summer afternoon, and his dad would be standing there in the yard, holding a football. A really nice new one, straight from the sporting goods store. Not a worn-out, half-flat one from the Salvation Army.

"Think quick, champ!" his dad would call, and he'd loft the ball to Dale. A perfect spiral pass. And Dale would make a perfect catch and run through all his brothers and sisters and score a touchdown. And then his father would grab him and hug him and go, "Here's the champion! The first eleven-year-old all-pro receiver in history!" And all his brothers and sisters would cheer. And then they'd play touch football until the sun went down. And then his dad would grill Polish sausages on the Weber in the backyard. And they'd all eat together and laugh and laugh. And then when it was time for bed, he'd have his own bed in his own room.

For some reason, today, his normal life dream hit him the moment he sat down in the car. The whole thing was so vivid in his imagination today—the colors, the smells, the feel of his dad's arms going around him—that Dale was trembling. It just kept going around and around and around in his mind.

After a minute he realized that he was still clutching the last stolen sausage link in his hand. The grease had dripped on his leg, congealing on his knee.

He hurled the sausage out the window.

Unfair! It was so unfair! Why did other people get such nice lives? And his was such a bunch of . . . ick. He had always felt like he deserved better. But today he had the strongest feeling. Like there was some other life that he was *supposed* to have. He could almost touch that other life, smell it, taste it. Memories of happy things that had never happened—that never *would* happen—had snagged like fishhooks in his brain. It was torture.

Dale put his head against the steering wheel and closed his eyes. He felt like crying.

XII

Jessica didn't know what to do. The only thing she could think of was to go to Dale's house. She was relieved to see that nothing had changed there. It was the same miserable-looking little white frame house, with the same weedy yard and the same peeling paint.

She walked up on the porch and knocked on the door. After a moment the door opened and a woman looked down at her curiously. It took Jessica a couple of seconds to recognize her.

"Mom?" Jessica said.

Her mom looked exactly the same. And yet, somehow, totally different. Instead of her usual neatly pressed button-down shirt and her usual neat gray skirt, her mother was wearing a pair of worn pink sweatpants, faded pink terry-cloth slippers, and a faded pink T-shirt that said SWEEEET! on the front.

"Why did you knock?" her mother said. Her voice seemed more shrill, more harried than normal. "The freakin' door's open."

"Mom?" Jessica said again. "What are you doing here?"

Her mother stared at her. "What does it look like I'm doing?" She pointed at a vacuum, which lay on the floor in a puddle of dust. "I'm trying to freakin' vacuum the freakin' floor, but the freakin' vacuum doesn't freakin' work and we can't freakin' afford another one because your freakin' father doesn't have a freakin' *job!*"

"I heard that!" a voice said. Jessica's dad. He was sitting on the other side of the room on the couch, with a bottle of beer in his hand, watching professional wrestling on TV. He was her dad exactly. Except sadder-looking. And there was a large puckered scar on one of his temples, a scar that hadn't been there before.

Jessica just stood there.

"In or out!" her mother said. "In or out. Don't just stand there letting all the flies in Minnesota into my house."

Jessica walked tentatively inside Dale's house. Only . . . it was obviously not Dale's house anymore. All of their furniture was jammed into Dale's much smaller house. It was the same furniture as they'd had in her real house. Only shabbier and dirtier.

Jessica's mother turned on the vacuum. It emitted a terrible, high-pitched whine, then a cloud of dust blew out all over the room. Jessica's mother picked up the vacuum and slammed it down on the floor. "I can't take this!" she shouted. "Nothing works in this house! Everything's falling apart! I can't take it! I can't take it anymore!" She slammed the vacuum into the floor again and again, swinging it around, knocking over lamps and vases. Finally the vacuum made a shattering noise and quit working completely.

The gnawing, sick feeling that Jessica had gotten when she had realized that the Ellises were living in her house suddenly got worse. She'd never seen her mother do anything like this in her life. Jessica's mom was ordinarily polite and calm to a fault. And she sure never used the word *freakin'*.

Jessica's father, meanwhile, just stared at the wrestling show on TV, motionless. A bead of water ran down the side of his beer, dripped onto the floor. It was barely lunchtime . . . and he was drinking a *beer?* Weird. Her father never drank before five o'clock. Not like Dale's dad, who seemed to have a beer in his hand all day.

Finally Jessica's mother put her face in her hands and began crying. The room was a wreck now, dust everywhere, furniture knocked over.

On the TV a huge veiny monster of a guy in a tight-fitting wrestler outfit was going, "I'm gonna crush you, Samoa Joe! I'm gonna tear yur head off and spit down yur neck, I'm gonna hurt you so bad yur unborn grandchildren are gonna cry. I'm gonna—"

"It's going to be okay, Mom," Jessica said.

Jessica's mother had collapsed into a chair, her head in her hands. "Not if the King of the Couch doesn't get up off his duff and get a job," her mother whimpered.

"Blah blah-blah blah-blah blah-*blah*," her dad drawled, never taking his eyes off the TV.

There was a knock at the door. Jessica's heart jumped. Maybe it was Dale!

She flung open the door. But it wasn't Dale.

It was a handsome-looking young guy with lots of gel in his hair so that it kind of stuck up off his head. He was smiling broadly, showing off a set of perfect teeth. In his hand was a large suitcase. "Look at *you!*" he said, tousling her hair. Then he pushed past her into the room. "I perceive I'm just in the nick, huh?" he said brightly, pointing at the wrecked vacuum cleaner on the floor.

Jessica's mother looked up at him. "What?" she said. "Who are you?"

"Bob Robbins Junior!" the young guy said. "I'm here for the one o'clock appointment."

"The *what?*"

The smiling young man reached inside his sport jacket, pulled out a business card, which he thumped twice with his middle finger, then set on the coffee table in front of Mrs. Sternhagen. The way he manipulated the card reminded her of a magician doing card tricks—like it was something he'd practiced for a long time in front of a mirror.

"Bob Robbins Junior," the man said, repeating his name. "Pow-R-Kleen Vacuum Corporation! The one o'clock appointment?"

Mrs. Sternhagen looked at him with dull, resentful eyes. "You didn't have any one o'clock appointment with me."

"Sure I did! Heck, it's right here in my doodad." He pulled a cell phone off his belt, poked the tiny buttons a couple of times, then turned it around so Jessica could see some kind of little calendar on the screen. "Yessiree! One o'clock. Right here in black and white."

"Oh," her mother said.

Jessica picked up the business card. It read:

✳ *Pow-R-Kleen Vacuum Corporation* ✳
(a subsidiary of Pow-R-Kleen Industries, Inc.)
· ·
Robert "Bob" Robbins Jr. · Senior Sales Consultant
"The Ick Just Goes Away!"

"The *ick*?" Jessica said. What a dorky slogan. It didn't even make sense.

"All the icky stuff," Bob Robbins said, smiling broadly at her. He spoke like a magician, reeling off some kind of singsongy spiel before he pulled the rabbit out of the hat. "All the mess, my friends. All the junk, the dust, the dirt, the grime, the grease, the crud, the gunk, the refuse, the litter, the disorder, the disarray, the misunderstandings, the sadness, the pain, the grief. You know . . . *ick*."

Was this guy serious? There was a big difference between grease and sadness. Jessica was going to say something sarcastic. But then she saw that her mother was nodding, like what Bob Robbins just said was totally genius.

Bob Robbins set his case on the coffee table, flipped it open. Inside was a collection of shiny red plastic parts. "A lot of people ask me, 'Bob, what's the best thing about the Pow-R-Kleen 5000?' And you know what I tell them? 'Nothing!'" He grinned and stood there, like he was waiting for Jessica's mom to say something.

Jessica's mother blinked but didn't speak. Bob Robbins started snapping the plastic parts together.

"I repeat. People ask me what's best about the Pow-R-Kleen 5000. And I say, 'Nothing.' Think I'm crazy, don't you? But, hey, consider this, Mrs. Sternhagen. What is it that makes pure filtered water taste so good? Why is clean, fresh air delightful to the nose? What is it that's so peaceful to the eye about the darkness between the stars? It's not about what's there; it's about what's *not* there. Am I right?"

Jessica's mother said nothing. She seemed content to just stare mutely at Bob Robbins, at his perfect smile, his manicured hair, his neat clothes.

"The reason I'm the number one Pow-R-Kleen salesman in the nation?" Bob Robbins flashed his white teeth. "Simple. I don't lie, I don't prevaricate, I don't tell tall tales, I don't slather on the hokum. I simply let the product speak." He finished snapping together the parts. And there was a red vacuum. "This, Mrs. Sternhagen, is—quite simply and without a shred, a hint, a particle, an *iota* of exaggeration—

the finest engineering achievement in the history of the world. Now I know what you're thinking, Mrs. Sternhagen. You're saying to yourself, 'That young man is a liar and a phony baloney.' Well, ma'am, just watch this."

He began vacuuming the room. Jessica scratched her head. She couldn't figure out what it was, but there was something amazing about it. It was like watching some movie star doing the most fabulous stunt you'd ever seen. He was almost inhumanly fast. And yet he seemed graceful, smooth, unhurried. Almost placid. There were all sorts of attachments and gizmos on the vacuum, and every few seconds he would snap on a new gizmo and then go back to cleaning. He vacuumed over papers without sucking them up, vacuumed the drapes without disturbing their folds, vacuumed cobwebs from the corners of the room without leaving marks on the walls—and yet managed to pull vast quantities of dust off the floor.

The demonstration took no more than a minute. And yet by the time he was done, there was not a speck of dust in the room. Not one. The room practically sparkled. And not only that, he had also somehow righted all the furniture that had been knocked over. Even the vase that had been broken was somehow miraculously fixed. The room, in short, was perfect.

"Look—" Jessica's mother said.

"It's not what's there, folks. It's what *not* there!" He made a broad gesture across the room. "The ick, my friends. Where is the ick? I'll tell you where. . . ." He patted the

Pow-R-Kleen 5000. "It's in here. Which is to say, it's gone. Adios, ick! Good riddance."

"But—" Jessica's mother tried to speak again.

"No filters, no bags, no messy parts to change. The ick is simply . . . *gone*." He snapped his fingers. "Gone."

"Yeah, but—"

Bob Robbins held up one finger. "Don't speak, ma'am. Not one word. Words, Mrs. Sternhagen, are the most precious things in the world. So don't waste a single one of them until you've heard, in its entirety, the extraordinary news I've brought to your home."

"Look here—"

"Ho! Woop! Nope! Not a word. Not yet." Bob Robbins sat on the couch next to Jessica's father. "Let me turn that down for you, sir," Bob Robbins said, grabbing the remote and turning down the television. Jessica's father made a face of disgust, then stood up and walked out into the kitchen. He had a strange, staggering hitch in his step, like something was bad wrong with his left leg. Or his balance. It was hard to tell. Jessica felt her guts clench up. Her father had never walked like that before. After a moment the back door banged shut.

"Mrs. Sternhagen, I know what you're thinking," Bob Robbins said. "You're thinking, 'Bob, that is indeed the finest vacuum I've ever seen in my life. But, Bob, I live in the crummiest little house on the crummiest street in town. Something went wrong down at the factory a couple of years ago and nothing has been the same in this household.' Yes? You're thinking, 'Bob, my dear husband here is on disability and spends his days glued to the couch watching professional wrestling, showing not a sign of ever getting a job again, and, frankly, therefore, Bob, the chances of my ever being able to afford this peerless piece of engineering are, in a word, zero.' Hm? Yes?"

Jessica's mother stared at the vacuum.

"You're also wondering, 'Bob, how does it work?' Well, frankly, Mrs. Sternhagen, I don't know. Using high-tech engineering principles, it creates a vortex of pure nothingness. And into that vortex goes all the . . . ick. Beyond that, I can't explicate the details. Gets into all kinds of physics and mumbo jumbo, and, Mrs. Sternhagen, frankly I'm not even a high school graduate. The whole thing's over my head."

Jessica's mother spoke for the first time. "Wow."

"But, Mrs. Sternhagen, listen closely because I've saved the best for last. What if I told you, Mrs. Sternhagen, that you could take possession of this vacuum, without obligation and absolutely without any cost to you? You would say, 'Bob, you're a liar.' Am I right?"

Mrs. Sternhagen was still looking at the vacuum. Her eyes glinted with a strange greed. Jessica had always thought that her mother didn't want a thing more than what they had. But now she seemed covetous and maybe even a little bitter, like something beautiful was being dangled in front of her, something she would never be able to have.

Bob Robbins Jr. grinned, showing his exceedingly white teeth. "Mrs. Sternhagen, lucky for you, the Pow-R-Kleen

Household Finance Corporation, a subsidiary of Pow-R-Kleen Industries, has just this week begun to offer to the public a financial product so revolutionary that it boggles the mind. This arrangement will allow you to assume possession of this engineering marvel at absolutely no cost to you."

"I can't afford another monthly payment," Jessica's mother said. "They repossessed the Ford just last week. Bill collectors are—"

"Mrs. Sternhagen, listen carefully please. This is not one of those shady pyramid schemes you've had the misfortune to get sucked into before. This is not a payment plan. This is not a come-on or a slick marketing gimmick. No, ma'am. Imagine for a moment, if you would, that you could defer all your financial obligations into the past."

Jessica's mother blinked.

"That's stupid," Jessica said. "To defer something means to push it into the future. Like, to put something off. You can't put something off into the past. That's a logical impossibility."

"A logical impossibility! Will you listen to this kid? The vocabulary! Wow!" Bob Robbins winked at her mother, then turned to Jessica, his voice dropping almost to a whisper, and said, "You know, Jess, sweetheart, I would think after everything that's happened to you today, you would understand that there's no such thing as logical impossibility." He turned back to Jessica's mom. "Mrs. Sternhagen, would you not agree this is the most amazing vacuum you've ever seen? And that it would restore to your home the order, hygiene, predictability, and certainty that you have so lacked since the unfortunate events that resulted in your living in this . . . well, let's be frank . . . in this miserable stinking rat hole of a house?"

Mrs. Sternhagen continued to stare raptly at the vacuum. She nodded vaguely.

"Excellent! Superb! Stupendous!" Bob Robbins clapped his hands together enthusiastically. "All that's necessary is that you approve the paperwork and I'll simply leave this entire vacuum cleaning system—including its handsome and durable carrying case—a two-hundred-dollar value, Mrs. Sternhagen, at no cost to you with this special one-day offer—plus the paper duster, the wall cleaner, the drapery attachment, the right-angle guide, and the carpet cleaning brush—right here in your home. How does that sound, Mrs. Sternhagen?"

Jessica's mother nodded mutely.

Bob Robbins Jr. patted his pocket. "Gosh, Mrs. Sternhagen, I seem to have misplaced my pen."

"I'll go get one," Mrs. Sternhagen said. There was a note of pleading and desperation in her voice. She stood up and disappeared into the kitchen, her pink slippers flapping on the linoleum.

The room was briefly silent. Bob Robbins smiled pleasantly and stared off into space. After a moment he began to hum softly. The song seemed extremely familiar.

And yet Jessica was sure that she'd never heard the song in her life.

"Who are you?" she said finally. "I mean, who are you really?"

The young man cocked his head. "Hm?"

"You heard me," Jessica said. "I don't think you really came here just to sell my mom a vacuum. Who are you?"

"Ah!" The young man smiled. "That. Yes. Well. If you must know . . ."

"Tell me."

He took out a pack of chewing gum, stuck a Juicy Fruit in his mouth, and chomped on it for a while, staring at her with amusement in his eyes. Finally he said, "I'm the villain."

Jessica frowned. "Huh?"

"*Her Lif!*" Bob Robbins said. "The book! Every book has to have a villain. Otherwise it would be completely boring and people would vomit when they read it."

Jessica scratched her head. "No," she said finally. "I don't think so. You seem like a creep. But not a villain."

"Why do you say that?"

"Because . . ." She thought about it. This whole thing with the vacuum seemed like some kind of weird joke. But it wasn't exactly scary. A villain would be scary. "I don't know," she said. "A villain wouldn't be a vacuum cleaner salesman. A villain would be like a . . ." She tried to think of an example.

"The leader of a country whose name you can't pronounce?" Bob Robbins said. "A guy with a German accent and a fancy car? Or perhaps a man with a shaved head and dirty words tattooed on his neck?"

"Maybe. But, mainly, a villain would do something bad. Not just sell stupid vacuums."

"I kind of resent your calling it stupid," Bob Robbins said. "It really *is* the best vacuum ever made." He cleared his throat. "But that's neither here nor there is it?" He stood up and opened the door. "You want me to do something bad? Come here for a sec."

She rose and walked to the door. She didn't really believe him. Bob Robbins seemed like a grown-up version of this kid in school, Larry O'Briant, who always talked in a loud voice about stuff that was so ridiculous and unbelievable that everybody knew he was lying the minute the words came out of his mouth. Larry O'Briant once told her that he had created a new form of life in an empty jar. Another time he said he had invented a jet engine that ran on cranberry-apple juice instead of jet fuel, and that the air force was going to pay him seventy-two million dollars for his brilliant design.

Bob Robbins pointed out to the street. Sitting at the curb was a white van, somewhat battered, with a sign on the side that said,

Pow-R-Kleen Industries
····· *"The Ick Just Goes Away!"* ·····

Bob Robbins waved at the van. Someone moved inside and then the back door of the van slid open. A large, muscular man climbed out. He was carrying a Pow-R-Kleen 5000 in his hand.

"Watch this," Bob Robbins said. "This is gonna be massively cool."

The muscular man started pushing the red vacuum across the street toward the house on the other side of the road. It was a blue-painted house with a motorcycle parked outside and a mean-looking dog chained up inside a chain-link fence. Loud music was booming out the windows. As soon as the muscular man started walking toward the house, the dog hurled itself at him, slamming into the fence. It began barking loudly, its tiny pink eyes fixed on the muscular man.

Immediately a disheveled guy with tattooed arms came out of the front door of the house and yelled, "Hey, you moron, stop bugging my dog!"

The muscular man flipped a switch on the vacuum. It emitted a soft, gentle whine.

As the whine got louder, the grass in front of the blue house across the street began to stretch and distort, like when you look at your face in a fun house mirror. Then the dog began to stretch, too. It stretched and stretched. Then suddenly it went *foop!* into the vacuum.

The tattooed man stared. "What the—"

"Nice, huh?" Bob Robbins Jr. said to Jessica.

"Hey!" the tattooed man screamed. "You gimme my dog back! You give it back or I'm gonna tear your head off and spit down your neck! I'm gonna hurt you so bad your unborn grandchildren are gonna—" Apparently the angry man had been watching the same wrestling show on TV as her father.

But then the angry man with the tattoos began to stretch, too. In about half a second—*foop!*—the angry man with the tattoos was gone, too. *Foop!*—and then the whole house. *Fooooooop!* The fence and the yard and the trees and the driveway. The muscular man turned off the vacuum.

Bob Robbins Jr. gave him a toothy grin and a big thumbs-up as the muscular man got back into the van and slammed the door.

Jessica felt sick. "Oh, God," she said.

"Is that villainous enough for you?" the salesman said.

"But where did they go?" Jessica said. There was no sign of the house now. Not even an empty lot. It was like the two houses flanking the blue house had simply moved closer together. As though the blue house had never existed at all.

"Give me the book and I won't do the same thing to your mom and dad," Bob Robbins Jr. said.

"But I don't—"

"I know you don't have the book at this precise moment. But you can get it. You're a clever little girl. And when you get it, I want it."

"Why?" Jessica said. "What's the big deal about that book?"

"Oh, I just want to be ruler of the entire known universe is all."

She looked at him through narrowed eyes, trying to envision him as some kind of Darth Vader–type guy, taking over the world. She still didn't quite see it. "Um . . . so how's my book supposed to help you do that?"

"All those weird people with the shadows in their eyes?" He slapped himself in the middle of the chest. "Mine. They're *my* people. *I* control them."

"What's that got to do with the book?"

"Well, I *do* control them. But, between you and me? I can only keep those morons under my thumb for a few minutes at a time. There's, ah . . . calibration issues, temporal bias compensation, things of that nature. Very technical. You wouldn't understand." He squinted thoughtfully at the ceiling. "Here, I'll make it nice and simple so a kid like you can understand it. With the power of your book on my side? Well . . . let's just say there won't be anything on this planet that will be able to stand in my way."

There was a sound of footsteps behind them, Jessica's mother shuffling out of the kitchen, her faded pink slippers flapping on the linoleum.

Bob Robbins Jr. leaned down toward Jessica and whispered, "Get me that book. Today. By five o'clock."

Jessica glared silently at him.

Bob Robbins Jr. turned and said, "Ah, Mrs. Sternhagen, perfect timing! I've got the paperwork all ready for you."

XIII

You will not believe what just happened!" Jessica said as Dale walked into the lobby of the library.

The short, balding man with the wince and the thick glasses still sat at the front desk reading a magazine. He looked up angrily. "Quiet!" he shouted.

Jessica noticed that Dale had a kind of odd expression on his face. He looked almost like he'd been crying. Which Dale never did, as far as she knew.

"Are you okay?" she said.

Dale shrugged. "I got chased off the factory property. Mr. Naami, the security guard—it's like he never even—"

"Quiet!" The Information guy was practically screaming at them.

Jessica looked at her watch. "Let's talk in a minute," she whispered. She was getting worried about the time. "The book must have fallen out of my bag when we were running away from all those people in the Map Room."

"Maybe we should ask him," Dale said. "He is the Information guy, after all."

And, in fact, a large sign hung over the desk saying:

·?·INFORMATION·?·

"Hm," Jessica said. The Information man seemed like he was in the wrong profession. He didn't seem like he enjoyed giving out information at all. But Dale was already walking toward him.

"Hi there!" Dale said as he approached the desk. "Us again, your favorite library patrons."

The man kept reading for a while, then finally stopped, put his finger in the magazine to hold his place, sighed loudly, and then looked up at them. "What," he said.

"Nice to see you again, too," Dale said brightly.

"We lost a book," Jessica said. "The one you looked up on the computer. Do you know where we should check to—"

"Circulation," the man said, opening his magazine and beginning to read again. He was reading *Pork Processing Monthly*. The title of the article was "Pep Up Your Kill Floor!" Jessica knew from her father that the kill floor was where the hogs were slaughtered.

"What's Circulation?" Jessica said.

The man looked back at the magazine and waved his hand in the direction of the desk where you checked out books. "Circulation," he said again.

"Oh! You mean the checkout desk?" Dale said.

The man sighed loudly again. "No, *not* the checkout desk,"

he said in a loud, condescending voice. "That's the word one might use if this were an elementary school library. In a *real* library, where grown-ups go, it's called *Circulation*."

"Neat-o!" Dale said. "Thank you for educating us on that truly important point of library terminology."

Jessica grabbed Dale's sleeve and pulled him away before he got them thrown out of the library. Still holding on to Dale's sleeve, she walked over to the checkout desk. "Is there, like, a lost-and-found place here?" she said to the person behind the checkout desk. "I lost a book."

The checkout person was a high school student. Jessica recognized him from church—though she couldn't remember his name. He had red hair and a very pointy nose. "You'll need to talk to Mr. Helgenberger," he said, pointing at a door behind the desk. "Just go through there."

They walked into the back room. A tall man with a long gray beard and a thin, kind face sat behind a very old desk. "Ah!" he said, smiling broadly. "Jessica!" Then he looked at Dale. "And you must be . . ." He snapped his fingers like he was trying to remember.

"Dale," Dale said.

The gray-bearded man scratched his head. "No, no, that's not it."

"I promise you, my name is Dale. Dale McDuffie."

"No, I really don't think that's it." The man shrugged. "Well . . . neither here nor there, neither here nor there. Please, sit!"

They sat. The chairs were covered in old, cracked leather, with lumpy springs in the seats that poked into Jessica's rear. "I'm trying to find this book that I lost."

"Yes, yes, I heard about that," the old man said thoughtfully. "Very worrisome." He turned and tapped some keys on his computer. "*Aspects of the Bluntwick Campaign*, right?"

"Excuse me?"

"The missing volume. The full name is *A Reexamination of Certain Aspects of the Bluntwick Campaign* by Sir Manfred F. C. Williams, right?"

"No. *Her Lif.* By Anonymous. Or maybe it's *Her Life.*"

One bushy eyebrow went up. "Oh. I could have sworn . . ." He tapped on the keys again. "Hm. *Her Life.* Yes. Well, I'm afraid it's still listed in the system as missing. Which means no one in my department has found it."

"Have you got any suggestions as to where else we might check?"

"You're sure it's not that book about the Battle of Bluntwick? Or perhaps du Bruguet's famous *Examination of the Battle of Bluntwick and*—"

"No!" Dale said, sounding exasperated.

The old man said, "Well, that's rather bad news, then, isn't it?"

"In what way?"

"Well . . ." Mr. Helgenberger reached into his pocket and pulled out a very old pocket watch. "If my timepiece is correct, then you have about six hours."

"Until what?"

"If that book got into the wrong hands . . ." He frowned and rubbed his beard nervously.

"What?" Jessica said.

"I thought somebody would have explained this to you?"

Jessica squinted at him, waiting.

"It's in all the future history books," Mr. Helgenberger said. "At roughly six o'clock tonight, Bob Robbins Junior is going to open a large . . . well, a sort of hole or tunnel between our universe and some other dimension. I'm not sure how it works, but at that point our entire universe will get sucked out the hole. Just like dirt into a vacuum cleaner. Fortunately you'll be there with the book to stop him." He stroked his beard again. "But . . . if you don't have the book, then . . ." His face went pale.

"The history of the future?" Jessica said. "That doesn't make sense."

Mr. Helgenberger stood, walked across the room. "Well, sometimes I do forget things. I'd better check." A long row of books bound in red leather sat on a shelf. He ran his finger down the spines until he found what he was looking for. "Ah! Here we are."

He picked up the book, cracked it open, and began scanning the page. Jessica could see the cover of the book. In gold letters it read,

A COMPLETE HISTORY OF THE FUTURE
❖IN SEVENTY-NINE VOLUMES *by* Roberto Rabel, Ph.D.❖

"Ah, here we go. Yes. 'At approximately one o'clock in the afternoon, Bob Robbins Junior inserted the device into a crack in the edge of the universe and turned on the device. By six o'clock the crack had transformed into a quaternary phase chronoplastic singularity' . . . blah blah blah. . . . 'Within seconds the universe was thoroughly cleaned, sucked through the crack and into another interstitial dimension where it was used for purposes that cannot be expressed in English—or, for that matter, any other human language. At one time it had been expected that Jessica Sternhagen would prevent this cleansing. But in the actual event—'"

The old man stared at the volume.

"Oh, dear," he said finally.

"What's wrong?" Jessica said.

"But I could have sworn that . . ." He pulled out volume after volume, opening them frantically and staring at the pages with obviously increasing distress. He reshelved the first couple of volumes. But after that he began simply dropping them on the floor.

Jessica picked up one of the books and looked at it. The pages were all blank. Volume after volume after volume. Apparently the future had pretty much ceased to exist. At least as far as these books were concerned. "Look, Mr. Helgenberger," she said, "if we can get *Her Lif* back, then we can stop this from happening."

The old man shook his head vaguely, then collapsed back into his chair. "It's in the book," he said feebly. "If it's in the book . . . there's nothing you can do."

"I don't believe that," Jessica said.

"Me neither," Dale said.

The old man looked around vaguely, like someone waking from a long nap. His hands were shaking as he tapped on the computer keys. "I can't help you," he said, an agitated expression on his face. "Your book is not in the system. Your book is, no, it's just not in the system."

"Then where do we go next?"

"Your book is not in the system." The old man's hands started to shake. "It's not in the system. The book's not in the system."

"Calm down!" Jessica said. "You have to have some kind of suggestion."

The man ran his fingers through his beard several times in a row. "Have you retraced your steps?"

"No," Jessica said. "But people were chasing us. They would have found it if we'd dropped it."

"And you're sure you had it when you came into the library?"

Jessica nodded.

"Sometimes strange things wash up in Ephemera."

"What's Ephemera?"

"It's one of our special collections. Subbasement four."

Jessica and Dale exchanged glances. "Last time we went down into those subbasements," Dale said, "we kinda didn't have a good time."

"What do you mean?"

"These weird people. It was like they had shadows in their eyes."

"Oh, dear, yes. Them. I'm guessing they won't bother you again, though," Mr. Helgenberger said. "At least not for a while."

"Why not?"

"From what I gather, it takes a huge amount of energy for them to do that. Once they finish, they have to store up energy again."

"Who does?"

"Well . . . we're not entirely sure who they are, honestly." The old man shuddered. "We believe they come from another dimension. They're the ones who are trying to tear a hole in the edge of the universe and swallow us up."

"But are they people? Or not?"

"They're not people, no. Not as we would know them. They can't actually have any physical presence in our universe. So they have to act through people. They take them over for a while."

Jessica suddenly had a creepy thought. "Why not just take *me* over, then?" Jessica said.

The old man shook his head. "No, they can only take over people who don't have a very strong sense of themselves. People who always are thinking how they'll appear to other people, always comparing themselves, always afraid that they aren't enough like other people? They're the ones they can take over. People like you are too strong."

Jessica frowned. "But I'm just a kid."

The old man looked at her sadly. "You are and you aren't," he said. Then he looked at his watch. "If you're going to have half a chance, you better go now. Ephemera. Subbasement four."

XIV

On the elevator Jessica was about to tell Dale about how her family had changed, and how she was living in his family's house—but Dale started telling her about hitting the security guard in the face with a piece of sausage . . . and somehow Jessica never got the chance to tell her story.

When they got to floor SB4, the same very large dog that had been there two hours earlier was still sitting there, staring at them through the brass grating of the elevator. The way the old elevator worked, they had to open the door themselves, folding it like an accordion. For a moment they just stood there, looking at the dog from behind the grating. On the wall behind the dog hung a large brass sign.

SPECIAL COLLECTIONS

Bluntwickiana	SB401
Philatelia	SB402
The Margarine Collection	SB403
Arabic Manuscripts	SB404

"Bluntwickiana?" Dale said. "What in the world is that?"

Jessica felt the hair standing up on her arms. She didn't mind dogs. But something told her this wasn't an ordinary dog. It just looked . . . well . . . scary. Unpredictable. "I don't know what Bluntwickiana is," she said. "But while that dog's sitting there, I'm not all that eager to find out."

The dog had odd yellow eyes and was nearly as tall as Jessica. A long string of drool hung from its mouth. It bared its teeth slightly and growled softly. Its teeth seemed unusually large—even for such a gigantic dog.

"I bet he's not that bad," Dale said. Dale loved dogs. "Some breeds are just scary-looking."

"You first," Jessica said.

Dale started to open the door. The dog growled and bared its teeth.

"Yeah," Dale said, slamming the door shut again. "Then again, maybe not."

"We have to get to that room, though," Jessica said, pointing. At the end of the long hallway behind the dog was a door, numbered B408.

"Look," Dale said. "There's a stairwell over there that

comes out next to the door of the Ephemera Room. Maybe we could go down one more floor and come back up."

Dale was right. The door to the stairs was close enough that they'd have a chance to make it. She stabbed the button for SB5.

The elevator began to shudder, and then the dog was gone. A few moments later, the elevator stopped at the next level.

Jessica eased the door open, peeped out. No giant slobbery evil dog. "Let's go," she whispered.

They got out of the elevator and looked around. The layout was different here. No hallway, no door to the stairwell.

In fact there was just a long wall with a single door in it, which read: PRINTING AND BOOKBINDING. STRICTLY NO ADMITTANCE.

"Crud," Jessica said.

Dale gave her a broad wink and pushed open the door.

Jessica followed. They found themselves in a huge, dim room. Large steel beams ran across the ceiling. Heavy, dark, clanking machines were scattered here and there throughout the large space. At the far end of the space was a large red door to what was obviously a stairwell.

"That's it!" whispered Dale, pointing at the stairs.

Unfortunately, before they could make another move, a man popped up from behind a nearby table and glared at them. He wore a large apron covered with ink, and his hair stuck up in a wild tangle.

"Can't you read?" he shouted. His face was beet red.

"Read?" Dale said, putting a comically idiotic look on his face. "You mean people come here to *read*?" He looked around blankly. "I was totally wondering why there were so many books in this building."

Before the man got even madder, Jessica jumped in and said, "Um, look, sir . . . we just wanted to get to the stairs over there."

"We just wanted to get to the *stairs*," the man said in a mincing, sarcastic voice. "Did it not occur to you that the reason there was a sign on the door saying 'strictly no admittance' was because we didn't want people traipsing through here?"

"Well—"

"And that maybe there was a *reason* for that? Maybe careless little kids could come in here and get their hands stuck in dangerous pieces of machinery or have their ears torn off or their legs amputated at the knee or their noses shredded or—"

"Okay, okay," Jessica said. "We get the point. But we can't go up in the elevator, so could we please use the stairs?"

The man put his hands on his hips. They were ink-blackened up to the wrists. "Absolutely not!"

"But we can't go up in the elevator."

"Is it broken?" He was actually trembling with anger.

"Um . . ."

The man made a face. "Oh! I thought not! Not broken at all, is it?"

"Actually . . . see we're supposed to go to Ephemera. But there's this huge dog in the way."

The man blinked and stared at them. The color drained from his face. "Dog?"

"A giant dog with these little yellow eyes and long teeth."

"Oh no . . . ," the man said softly. He rubbed the side of his face, leaving a long streak of black ink.

"What?" Jessica said. "What's wrong?"

The man was looking anxiously around the room now. He didn't seem too concerned with Jessica and Dale anymore. "Cerberus," he whispered.

"What?" Jessica said. "Who?"

But the man simply swept past them, ran out the door, slamming it behind him.

"Okay, that was weird," Dale said.

"What did he say?" Jessica said. "It sounded like he said 'Serberish' or something."

"Cerberus," Dale said. "In Greek mythology that's the three-headed dog that guards the river you have to cross to enter the land of the dead."

"Yay," Jessica said. "That's cheerful."

"Let's go," Dale said, heading briskly across the room, "before that guy comes back and smashes our faces in."

Jessica followed him toward the stairwell at the far end of the room. They wound their way around the big machines. Printing and binding machines, she assumed.

They had just about reached the stairwell when her eyes came to rest on something. Her heart jumped.

"Wait!" she said. "Dale!"

Dale stopped, his hands on the door to the stairwell. "What?"

"Look," she said.

There, on the table, lay a book. On the cover were the words *Her Lif*.

Dale snatched the book off the table, opened it. When he did so, all the pages fell out. At which point, it was obvious they weren't pages at all.

"That isn't even a book," Jessica said disappointedly. "It's just a stupid block of wood with a cover on it."

"No, it's a mock-up," a voice said. Jessica looked around with a start. A woman with short curly hair was standing beside the machine. She wore a name tag on her chest that said *elise martin*.

"A what?"

"A mock-up," Elise Martin said, smiling pleasantly. "We're rebinding a volume, and so we made the cover before the pages arrived. The wood block is just a form for us to make the cover on."

"You're rebinding *this* book?" Jessica said, holding up the empty cover.

"Yeah. A rush job," Elise Martin said. "The order was just called in this morning. The volume itself should be arriving any minute."

Jessica looked at Dale. "Who called the order in?" Dale said.

Elise Martin said, "What—you have a special interest in this book?"

"Yeah," Jessica said. "It's my book."

Elise Martin looked puzzled. She fumbled around with some papers that lay on the table. "No, I think the one I'm rebinding is owned by the library." She stared at the paper. "Yeah, this was called in by the director's office just a few minutes ago."

"The *director's* office?" Jessica was puzzled. If the director had found it, you'd think he'd have tried to make sure that he got it to Jessica. "By the director himself?"

"No. It was . . . well, actually it was Olaf, the janitor. But he said he was calling on behalf of the director."

There was a tremendously loud swishing and thumping noise. "Maybe this is it," Elise Martin said, pointing to a row of large pipes that descended from the ceiling. "This is our pneumatic book-delivery system. We can send books to and from any department with it."

The tubes reminded Jessica of the machine they used at the drive-through window at her mom and dad's bank, sucking the deposits up inside the building, using compressed air.

Elise Martin opened a small door with a lever and pulled out an ancient-looking cylinder or barrel made of brass and dark wood. The cylinder was about as big around as Jessica. She opened a small door in the barrel, revealing a stack of books. "No," she said. "Never mind, this is something different."

Jessica looked at the spines of the books to make sure. None of them were *Her Lif*.

Dale tugged on Jessica's arm and said, "Olaf? Why would that guy send the book up here? He's just the janitor."

"Yeah," Elise Martin said, frowning. "I thought that was a little odd, myself. He said the cover had been burned in a fire, but that otherwise the volume was fine. Said he'd be sending it right up."

"He must have found it after the incinerator cooled down!" Jessica said.

"Excellent!" Dale said, giving her a high five. "All we've got to do is sit here and wait for it."

"Or maybe we should just go down and get it from him."

"Don't you think it's a little weird, though?" Dale said. "Why didn't he give it to the director?"

Before she could think of an answer to his question, she heard a loud bang. They looked across the room. The man with the wild hair and the ink-stained hands had thrown the door open. "Run!" he shouted.

Jessica stared.

Before she had a chance to wonder why the man was running, she got her answer. The huge dog, Cerberus, was bounding through the door, barking angrily.

"Run for your lives!"

Dale grabbed Jessica's hand and yanked her toward the stairway door.

The dog's deep frenzied barking filled the room now, louder even than the clanking of the printing machines.

Dale grabbed the doorknob of the stairwell door and twisted it.

"Oh no!" Dale said.

"What?" she said.

Dale's face was stiff with terror. "It's locked!"

XV

Bob Robbins Jr. parked his van next to a Shoney's Big
Boy restaurant two blocks from the sausage factory.
"Put the new sticker on the van, Dingle," he said.

Wordlessly, his muscular assistant got out of the passen-
ger side of the van, peeled the sticker off the side that said
POW-R-KLEEN INDUSTRIES, and put a new, smaller one on the
door of the van. Inside a circle with an eagle on it were the
words UNITED STATES DEPARTMENT OF AGRICULTURE. Then,
underneath that, it said INSPECTION UNIT 49.

Two minutes later Bob Robbins was walking into the
front office of the sausage factory, where he flashed a
badge identifying him as a meat inspector for the United
States government. "I'll need to see the kill floor today, Mr.
Uhhh . . ."

"McDuffie," the man in the front office said, shaking
Bob Robbins's hand. "I'm Ed McDuffie. I'm the compliance
manager here at the factory."

The compliance manager wore a white hard hat and a
spotless white lab coat over a neatly pressed suit. He was

friendly and open-looking. The ideal kind of guy for what Bob Robbins Jr. had in mind.

Mr. McDuffie led Bob Robbins and his assistant through the factory, which smelled of rotting meat and disinfectant.

"Kind of unusual," McDuffie said, "your being here today. That other fellow just did an inspection last week."

"We've got a new district manager," Bob Robbins said. "Between you and me, he's a horse's patoot. Real stickler, this guy. He'll never last. Meantime, though, I'd be watching your p's and q's."

"Oh, yeah?"

"That's a fact," Bob Robbins said. "That is, indeed, a fact."

Ed McDuffie looked over at Dingle and said, "What's with the vacuum cleaner?"

"Looks like a vacuum cleaner, doesn't it?" Bob Robbins Jr. said. "Fact of the matter, though, it's some new gizmo for collecting test samples. Airborne contaminant levels or something. Be honest with you, I don't even know what it does. All I know, the new district manager wants us to deploy it pronto. Right, Dingle?"

The assistant nodded.

"Don't talk much, does he?" the man in the white lab coat said, smiling.

"Been with me a week and a half, hasn't spoken three words to me yet," Bob Robbins said. "Right, Dingle?"

"Four," Dingle said.

"I stand corrected," Bob Robbins said, chuckling loudly as they entered the kill floor. It was a giant space about the size of a football field. At one end, squealing pigs came through a chute. They were hoisted up on steel hooks and then killed. A line of the dead pigs moved swiftly through the room, hanging from the hooks. The smell was incredibly horrible.

"So . . ." McDuffie said, smoothing down the front of his white lab coat.

Bob Robbins pointed. "We're gonna set this gizmo up at the far end of the room. You may notice something funny when it comes on. But it's nothing to worry about." He smiled broadly. "Trust me."

"Funny?" the man in the white lab coat said. "Funny how?"

Bob Robbins Jr. looked at Dingle. "How would you put it, Dingle?"

Dingle just shrugged. They reached the far side of the room, and Dingle plugged the vacuum cleaner into a socket along the wall. "This okay, Ed? Just want to make sure it's not in your way."

Ed McDuffie shrugged. "Should be okay."

"Excellent!" Bob Robbins Jr. nodded at Dingle, who flipped the switch. In the din of squealing pigs, it wasn't even possible to hear the machine come on.

Ed McDuffie peered at the vacuum cleaner. "I don't see anything funny."

Bob Robbins pointed at the floor. There it was, next

to the vacuum cleaner—a black spot, like a tiny drop of black ink had fallen on the floor right next to one of the machine's red plastic wheels. It was no bigger around than a pencil lead.

Ed McDuffie leaned over and squinted at it. On closer inspection it didn't look like ink after all. "What is it?" he said. "Looks almost like a hole in the floor."

He stuck his finger out to touch it.

"Actually?" Bob Robbins said sharply. "Wouldn't do that if I were you."

Ed McDuffie hesitated, his finger just above the little spot or hole or whatever it was. He had a funny look on his face. "I just had the weirdest feeling," he said, finally pulling his finger away. "Like I'd been here before."

"Déjà vu," Bob Robbins Jr. said.

"Yeah." Ed McDuffie scratched his head. "Except it was like the other time I was here, something really bad happened." He looked around vaguely, blinking, like somebody was shining a really bright light in his eyes. "You know what? All of a sudden I'm feeling a little queasy right now. I think I'll let you fellows finish up here and then see yourselves out."

He walked away, shaking his head.

Meanwhile, Dingle was busy stringing yellow caution tape around the vacuum cleaner. When he was done, he hung an official-looking plastic sign on the wall that said:

EVIDENCE COLLECTION DEVICE
⚡ DO NOT TOUCH!!! ⚡

**Tampering with this device is a violation
of USDA code IV/33/109B**

Subject to a maximum fine of $50,000 and/or
one (1) year of imprisonment.

"You do fine work, Dingle," Bob Robbins said.

With that, they turned and walked out of the factory.

By the time they had reached the parking lot, the hole in the floor (if that's what it really was) had grown to the size of a match head.

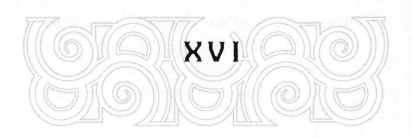

XVI

The giant dog bounded across the floor toward Jessica, Dale, and the bindery worker, Elise Martin. Dale wrestled furiously with the door handle to the stairwell. But it did no good.

It seemed to Jessica that the whole world had gone into slow motion. The dog was flying through the air, leaping tables and chairs and machines. But—though she was very frightened—she found, to her surprise, that she seemed to be thinking very calmly and quickly. It was clear to her that they could not get out the door. And there were no other doors in the room—other than the one through which the huge dog had come.

She scanned the room, looking for a place to hide.

Unfortunately, there just wasn't one.

The closest cover was the large binding machine. But it would only give them temporary shelter. The dog would just chase them around the machine until it caught them.

Which left nothing but the huge pneumatic tubes hanging from the ceiling.

She grabbed Dale's hand. "Forget the door," she said.

Dale followed her as she sprang onto the table by the tubes.

"What!" Dale said.

The dog was coming closer and closer, its teeth flecked with foam. Its eyes were pinned on her face.

"Get in the tube!" she shouted.

"Huh?"

There wasn't time to tell him again. She simply shoved him into a tube. Next to the tube was a large brass button that said SEND.

"He can't get in there!" Elise Martin shouted frantically. "He might be killed."

And Dale shouted, "This is crazy! What if I get stu—"

There wasn't time to think about it. Jessica slammed the SEND button with her palm. There was a loud rushing sound, and Dale's hair suddenly stood up straight on his head.

And then he was gone.

Elise Martin stared at the empty tube. But Jessica wasn't concerned about her. She was worried about the dog.

The dog's yellow eyes and foam-flecked teeth grew closer and closer.

There was still air rushing into the pneumatic tube. Jessica knew she couldn't get in until Dale had reached his destination. There was just no time to wait.

In desperation she squeezed into the tube next to the one Dale had entered. It was slick brass, polished smooth from years of use. There was a metallic smell. The dog was only about thirty feet away now.

"Help!" she called to Elise Martin, her voice echoing in the brass tube. "Press the button!"

But Elise Martin had turned her attention to the dog. She stared at it in horror.

"Ma'am! Please press the button!"

Still the woman didn't move. For a moment Jessica thought she was too late. Finally she reached out, her fingers stretching toward the button. She couldn't quite reach it. The dog was only one bound away.

Her fingers touched the button. She wriggled and lunged slightly, felt the button yield. As the mouth of the huge beast filled her vision, she heard a rushing noise like a thousand freight trains, and a strange pressure grabbed her. She realized that she was larger than Dale. What if she got stuck? Her hair flew straight up, and the pressure built until it felt like her brains would get sucked out the top of her head.

As the dog's huge teeth clanged against the sides of the tube, she realized she still hadn't had a chance to tell Dale about how the universe had changed. It was at that moment that something struck her, something she hadn't even thought about. If she was living in Dale's house . . . then where was Dale's family living?

And then she rocketed upward into blackness.

XVII

Jessica flew up and up and up through the darkness. Then suddenly the pipe twisted several times. With each twist, she felt herself wedged tighter and tighter into the pipe, and her head and elbows and knees banged into the hard brass.

Now she was hurtling along sideways. *Thump!* As the pipe dipped, her head hit the side so hard her ears rang.

And then suddenly she was upside down, hurtling downward. She wasn't able to put her hands over her head. She imagined crashing headfirst into something and flattening her head like a pancake.

But then suddenly the rushing sounds stopped and her progress slowed. She saw a tiny crack in the side of the pipe—light spilling through. She came to a dead stop.

There was a brief hiss. And then silence.

Suddenly the door to the pipe flew open and a pair of hands grabbed hold of her.

"How strange!" a voice said. "This doesn't feel like a book at all. It feels like a little girl!"

Jessica unfolded herself as the hands continued to pat

her body. It didn't hurt, but it seemed very odd. "Um? Where am I?" she said.

She looked up and saw a very beautiful woman wearing black clothes, a black wool hat, and black sunglasses. She had very long blond hair—almost as blond as Jessica's. "The question is, *Who* are you?" the woman said.

"Jessica Sternhagen," she said.

"Jessica Sternhagen!" the woman said. "No kidding?"

"Yeah, I was being chased by this dog and I had to get away. So I came through the pneumatic doohickey. Where am I?"

"You're in the Braille Room, of course. I'm Miss Star, the librarian for the blind."

Which is when Jessica realized that the librarian couldn't see. She had been running her hands over Jessica in order to "see" the strange thing that had just popped out of the pneumatic chute. Jessica looked around and saw that there were a number of people seated at tables, all of them running their fingers across the pages of braille books and magazines.

Jessica realized what she needed to do next. She climbed off the table in front of the pneumatic tubes and said, "Could I use your phone?"

"Of course, sweetie. It's right here." The librarian pushed a phone toward Jessica.

"Do you have a listing of people in the library? I want to call the janitor."

The woman ran her finger down a piece of paper taped to the desk next to the phone. There was nothing written on it, but it was covered with tiny braille bumps. "It's extension four-seven-two."

Jessica dialed and waited. After a moment a man said, "Hello?"

"Hi, Olaf. This is Jessica Sternhagen, the girl you met this morning. Did you find that book that we were looking for?"

There was a brief pause. "What book?"

"I just talked to the lady in the binding room. She said you called her and wanted her to rebind *Her Lif*—that book that we were afraid got burned up in the incinerator."

"Uh-huh."

Jessica waited. Olaf didn't say anything else.

"Uh-huh *what*, Olaf?" she said finally. "Did you find the book . . . or didn't you?"

"I guess I must have," he said.

"Well, I need it right now," Jessica said. She was getting a little frustrated.

Another long pause.

"Olaf, do you have the book?"

Olaf grunted. "Uh. Hm. Yeah, no, I guess I don't really remember." She heard a scratching noise, like he was scratching his hair or his face. "I feel kinda funny. Like my head ain't working right."

"Look around you. Do you see a book, Olaf?"

"Uh . . . There's kinda a bunch of books here. It's a library, you know?"

"Okay. But this is a very old book. And I think the cover got burned in a fire. Do you see a book like that?"

"Oh!" Olaf suddenly sounded happy. "Yeah. There it is."

"Can you get it? I need you to get it and hold on to it for me until I come down to where you are. Can you do that?"

"I'm not sure."

"Why not?"

"Well . . . 'cause of where the book's at?"

"Where would that be?"

"There's this dog, see? And it's got the book in its mouth. And it don't look like it would be all excited if I took that book from its mouth."

Jessica felt a stab of fear. "Oh no!" she said.

"Uh-oh!" Olaf said. "There he goes."

"He's gone? With the book?"

"Yup. Afraid so."

Frantically Jessica tried to think what to do next. "Olaf, is there any way for that dog to get out of the basement besides the stairs or the elevator?"

"Nope," Olaf said. "Ain't no other way out."

"Thanks," Jessica said. She hung up the phone, then turned to the blind librarian. "I need to call the director now."

"That's three-oh-oh," the librarian said.

Jessica punched the buttons rapidly. "Hi! It's Jessica," she said when the director answered. "Do you have a security guard or something? This huge dog has the book. It's in one of the subbasements. If you can close off the elevator and the stairs, we can trap it!"

"Good work! I'll meet you in the lobby," the director said. The line went dead.

Jessica ran out the door of the Braille Room and found herself on the second floor of the building. A large marble staircase led down to the lobby. She ran down the stairs. As she did so, she saw two security guards running across the lobby toward the elevator. By the time she reached the lobby floor, the director was emerging from his office, too.

"Shut down the elevator!" the director yelled to the guards. "It'll have to take the stairs."

One of the guards pulled a large ring of keys off his belt, selected a large brass key, inserted it into a keyhole in the wall next to the elevator, then rapidly turned the key.

They all waited tensely at the door to the stairwell.

Nothing happened.

After a moment the director turned to Jessica and said, "So how did you find out about the book?"

"I was in the binding room and the woman who worked there said she'd gotten an order for a book to be rebound. She already had a mock-up made."

"And Olaf made the order?"

Jessica nodded. "He said you told him to do it."

The director frowned. "How strange. I never told him to do that."

"Then the dog came into the binding room. Dale and I escaped through the pneumatic tubes."

The director's eyes widened. "You could have been killed!"

"You didn't see that dog," Jessica said. "Going through the tube seemed a lot less scary than being attacked by that dog."

"Hm," the director said. He turned to the guards. "You hear anything from the stairwell?"

The guard with the key chain opened the stairwell door tentatively, listened, then shook his head. "Nothing."

They waited some more.

"So where did you come out of the pneumatic tube?" the director said.

Jessica pointed. "The Braille Room. Up there."

The director looked puzzled.

"You know," Jessica said, "the room for blind people?"

"Um . . ." he said finally. "We don't have a Braille Room."

Jessica felt her heart sink. "Then what . . ."

Before she could finish her thought, one of the security guards cocked his head and said, "I hear something."

Jessica heard it, too. A soft clattering noise, like the nails of a dog. They were getting louder and louder.

XVIII

Dale came to rest with a jerk. Upside down. In the dark.

He waited for a moment, then called out: "Hello? Hello? Anybody there?"

After a moment there was a scrabbling sound, then the side of the pipe opened and light flooded in. Dale found himself staring up into the upside-down face of a beefy man. If the man hadn't been wearing a brown suit, he would have looked like a wrestling coach. He wore a plastic tag on his jacket pocket, but Dale couldn't read it upside down.

Dale wanted to find Jessica as quickly as possible. Had she gotten away from the dog? "Thanks," he said as he tried to clamber off the table.

But the man who looked like a wrestling coach grabbed hold of his shoulder. "Where do you think you're going, young man? Those tubes are not for joyriding."

"Let go of me!" Dale struggled, but the man was very strong. He held on with one hand, then used the other to dial the phone. Dale could read the tag on his coat now. It said that he was Mr. Dinwiddie, special collections librarian. The guy looked like the last person in the world to be a librarian.

"I'm calling security," the big man said. "We've had enough of you hooligans breaking in here and messing around with our collection."

"But I really have to go!" Dale said desperately.

Mr. Dinwiddie ignored him. Since he couldn't get away, Dale stopped struggling and looked around the room. There was a big sign on the wall that said EPHEMERA COLLECTION. There were all kinds of weird old posters on the wall—circus performers, dancers, clowns, magicians. All of them looked like they were a zillion years old.

Once Dale stopped trying to get away, Mr. Dinwiddie let go of him. Sensing an opportunity to escape, Dale immediately made a break for the door.

"I really wouldn't do that," the big librarian said.

Dale grabbed the door and started to open it. But then he froze. Standing there in the middle of the hallway was the huge dog with the yellow eyes. Dale slammed the door shut and retreated back into the Ephemera Room.

The librarian stroked his face. "Wait a minute," he said, frowning. "You're Dale McDuffie, aren't you?"

Dale nodded.

"The door's locked so the dog can't get in. But there's no back door out of here, so we're going to have to stall until we can find a way of getting rid of it."

"Maybe you should call Animal Control."

The man smiled. "I don't think Animal Control could handle that dog. We'll have to think of something else. Meantime, I've got a project for you."

"A what?"

"A project. Follow me."

Dale followed the man over to a long row of filing cabinets. "I'm Irvin Dinwiddie," he said, "curator of Ephemera."

"Hi," Dale said.

"Let me explain a little about the Ephemera collection," the librarian continued. "*Ephemera* means 'things that don't last.' In our case, it means printed matter that was made to be thrown out. Posters, catalogs, theatrical programs, handbills, things of that nature. Most of the items in our collection are over a hundred years old. Some much older."

"Okay."

"This is a collection of extremely rare posters related to magicians and conjurers. Last week some little snot-nosed moron broke in here and messed them all up. When you popped out of the pipe over there, I assumed it was you. My apologies. Anyway, notwithstanding the fact that it wasn't you who messed them up, I could use some help getting them reorganized. Since you're stuck here, I'll let you help out. I need them organized. Sort them by date, if you'd be so kind."

"But I really need to—"

"There are no coincidences in the world, young man," the librarian said sharply. "There's information here that you need to be aware of. Might as well make yourself useful."

Dale's eyes flicked toward the window into the hallway again. The dog was sitting with its face up against the glass, staring directly at him, two small circles of condensation forming on the window next to its nostrils. It had something clamped in its mouth that Dale couldn't quite make out.

Dale looked away nervously and started flipping through the pile of posters. They were so old that they felt like they might crumble in his hands. The colors were faded.

"Ah, there's an extraordinarily rare one," the librarian said.

The poster Dale was holding showed a man with a pencil-thin mustache and a very wide, insincere smile. He was holding a magic wand and wore a black cape and a top hat. It said: VICTOR THE MAGNIFICENT MOLDAVIAN CONJURER! *Watch him make animals, children, etc. disappear!* The picture was very crude . . . and yet there was something about the man's face that seemed familiar.

"That one's from 1854," Irvin Dinwiddie said. "But the next one is a great deal rarer."

"This little poster here?" Dale said. The next one was a flimsy, worm-eaten piece of paper, printed in black ink.

"Strictly speaking it's not a poster. It's a handbill. They were handed out by touts in London to attract customers." Dale was not sure what a *tout* was. But it didn't really matter. The handbill read:

❖ Victor the Moldavian ❖

"Moldavia," Irvin Dinwiddie said, "is a country that's between Russia, Poland, and Romania. We have ephemera stretching over a period of more than two hundred years featuring a mysterious Moldavian magician who makes animals and children disappear. Isn't that odd?"

Dale shrugged.

"He makes his first appearance in 1703. Isn't that an interesting coincidence?"

"I don't know. Is it?"

"What happened in 1703?" Irvin Dinwiddie said insistently.

Dale shrugged. "I have no idea."

"The Battle of Blunkovich. Known in English as the Battle of Bluntwick? Hm? Ring a bell?"

Dale frowned. "Now wait a minute," he said. "All day I keep hearing about this stupid Battle of Bluntwick. But I've read a lot of history books . . . and before today I never once heard of any Battle of Bluntwick."

Irvin Dinwiddie cocked his head. "I guess you must have skipped that chapter in the history books."

Dale scowled. This was just dumb. Dale was kind of a nut about history. And he'd never in his life heard about any Battle of Bluntwick.

"Anyway, that's not important," the librarian said. "But here's something for you to read."

He pushed a very old book across the table. "Read this," he said quietly. "Start on page seventy-four. I'm going to go over to my desk and try and figure out a way to distract that thing in the hallway so I can get you out of here."

"Uh. Okay." The image of the dog flashed through Dale's mind.

Derwood Jergensen had been working at the sausage factory for seven years now. In all those seven years, nothing interesting had ever happened. Not once. Pigs came in one end of the factory and sausage came out the other. In between, a lot of smelly, messy, disgusting things happened. But . . . interesting? No, not interesting.

Today, though? Today, something interesting happened.

Derwood Jergensen's job was to run the trotter vat. *Trotter* was the word used in the pork processing industry for pigs' feet. All the pigs' feet got chopped off on one end of the kill floor. Then the feet came down a conveyor belt and went into a vat, where they got cleaned. Every now and then there'd be a big clump of pig trotters on the belt, and one or two of them might get jammed and fall off onto the floor. When that happened Derwood would just pick them up, hose them off, and chunk them into the vat.

Derwood found this part of his job to be annoying. He had gained a little weight over the past few years and his belly had gotten bigger, so he had to grunt and strain whenever he leaned over. Derwood was not into grunting and straining.

So today a big clump of trotters came down the line, and when they reached the vat, one of them fell off onto the floor. Derwood sighed and looked at it, deciding whether or not he should stoop over to pick it up. What he had found was that if you accidently (but actually somewhat on purpose) kicked the trotters, they'd sometimes end up in another part of the factory. And then they would be some-one else's problem. He looked around to see if anybody was paying attention. They weren't. So he kicked the pig foot. It went skittering across the cement floor toward the area that had been cordoned off by the U.S. government meat inspector.

And then it just sort of disappeared.

Derwood frowned and walked over to see what had happened. When he got closer, he realized it hadn't actu-ally disappeared. It had simply fallen down a hole. The hole was perfectly round, inky black, and about as big around as a soup bowl. Just big enough for a pig's trotter to fall into. He looked down into the hole. He couldn't see any-thing.

He couldn't get too close to it, though, because it was behind the yellow caution tape. There was a big official-looking sign from the federal meat inspectors saying how you weren't supposed to mess with anything behind the tape. He wanted to get closer, but they made a big deal at the factory about never doing anything to make the federal inspectors mad, so he figured he better not cross the tape.

He went back to the line and found that two more trotters had hit the floor. He kicked them viciously toward the hole. Once again, they seemed to simply vanish as soon as they hit the hole.

Which was perfect, really.

For the entire shift, Derwood just kept kicking all the fallen trotters in the hole. It was only when he got back from his lunch break that something struck him. The hole had gotten bigger.

Not just a little bigger. A lot bigger. It was now about the size of a manhole cover. He went over and looked in for the second time. It was inky black inside the hole, like nothing he'd ever seen before. Was it some kind of sinkhole or something?

He shivered. Something about it gave him the heebie-jeebies. He stared for a long time. Should he go tell the shift foreman?

As he was pondering the question, he thought about all those pig trotters he'd kicked into the hole. It'd be hard to explain things to the bosses if they sent some joker down the hole and he finds a big honking pile of trotters down there, huh? Derwood shrugged and went back to work.

If the thing was a problem, somebody would sort it out eventually. No point getting involved.

Dale began reading the book that the librarian had given him. It was extremely old, printed on heavy paper that looked like it was ready to turn to dust and blow away in the next big wind. But then, Dale supposed, there weren't a lot of big winds blowing through the Ephemera collection. The book only had about six or seven pages.

It was called *A True Relation of the Coronation of the King of Poland Including Certain Unusual Features & Cetera & Cetera*. It was dated 1703.

The book began this way:

⟫◇⟪

His Majesty, Janosch III, having lain two nights in the castle of the Bishop of Cracovia, on the thirtieth of June, he made his entry into the city center in the following way: viz. First, one hundred and eighteen ensigns were borne in a stately manner by Soldiers clothed in blue, followed by six companies of foot dressed in red, having blue Caps. Those preceded six companies of Latvian foot soldiers clothed in green with yellow caps. There followed two troops of cavalry, the first dressed in the manner of Poland, the second in the manner of Germany, both very richly and superbly mounted. All those were followed by two troops of hussars with white and blue coats and high boots of the finest black leather.

⟫◇⟪

It went on like this for a while, listing all the soldiers and marshals and senators and ambassadors and dukes and so on who went in front of the king as he rode in this big parade to where he was about to be crowned king. After a bunch of pages of this . . .

—————◆—————

The King appeared afterward mounted on a dapple gray horse, under a canopy borne up by six senators: and His Majesty did not so much appear King by the tokens of his Office, but by the lofty and warlike countenance whereby he distinguished himself from his fellow nobles. This Great Prince's Habit was of pearl gray cloth trimmed with gold, with a crimson cap upon his head furred with Zebolina, and on it a black feather adorned with several great Pearls and Diamonds of great value.

—————◆—————

Then more about the big parade and his clothes and all the high muckety-mucks who fussed over him and so on. It was semi-interesting . . . but after a while Dale started feeling like he was reading a three-hundred-year-old version of *People* magazine. Lifestyles of the rich and famous. Big whoop.

Dale looked up to see if the dog was still there. It was. Still staring straight at him.

"What about the police?" Dale called to the beefy librarian. "Couldn't they get rid of him?"

"Keep reading," the librarian said. "I'll sort out the dog situation."

But then the librarian didn't do anything. He just sat

there, working a crossword puzzle, a stub of pencil nestled in his beefy fingers. Dale was starting to feel a little irritated. But what could he do? He started reading again.

❖

At the entrance to the city, and several other instances where His Majesty was to pass, were erected Triumphal Arches on which were depicted scenes representing the Battel and famous Victory over the S_____ at Bluntwick: or as it is styled in Poland, Blunkovich. Thus he passed to the Cathedral wherein the Prince was crowned Monarch of the realm by the Bishop according to the ancient Traditions of the Polish.

Thus concluded, the procession, still admirably constituted, passed back whence it came. Upon reaching the Castle, His Majesty dined upon pheasants, partridges, hares, suckling pigs, sausages, oryxes, venison, ibexes, goose, snipe, mutton, beef, and all manner of other fine meats. Whilst dining, the King and his Party were regaled by an Orchestra playing music in the German manner, composed for the occasion by Maestro Adolph-Joachim Kranz. After the conclusion of the feast, were several other Entertainments staged, including a Contest between a lion and a Giant Dog: which—to the surprise of All—resulted in the utter Conquest of the lion, as well as a theatrical drama of commendable Pomp and Gravity recounting the events of the Battel of Bluntwick. Last came a Magician, a grave and formidable man, styled Victor the Moldavian, who, to the wonderment even of His Majesty, suffered the Giant Dog, a contrabass viol, a trumpet, the magician's assistant, & cetera, to vanish into a Peculiar Hole which he opened in the Earth. Lastly, the Conjurer himself disappeared: the Hole in the ground closing up around him after his Exit. Outside of the city, it is said that as the hole closed, flocks of birds burst into flame and dropped from the air.

⊰ F I N I S ⊱

⊱━━◆━━⊰

And that was the end of it.

As Dale set the little book down, the librarian looked up. "Have you got them organized yet?"

"Uh . . . not quite."

"Keep at it," the librarian said. "Then tell me what changes."

Dale started putting the posters in order. He wasn't sure what Irvin Dinwiddie was talking about. But then he saw it. In 1874, the posters changed. Before, they had all been advertising Victor the Moldavian. Then, suddenly, in 1874, it was Babu the Moldavian. He flipped quickly through the posters. Victor, Victor, Victor . . . then, boom, Babu, Babu, Babu.

"So what happened to Victor?"

"Read the article at the end."

Dale looked at the bottom of the pile. There he found a crumbling newspaper article dated January 9, 1874. The headline read:

STRANGE
OCCURRENCE
❈ IN THEATER ❈

Minneapolis—Yesterday, in a most peculiar performance, a conjuror's magic appears to have been too powerful for his own good.

Appearing in his third performance at the Hejaz Theater on Thursday, Victor the Moldavian inexplicably disappeared.

At the climax of the show, after making a pig, a chicken, and a pocket chronometer disappear into a hole in the floor, the magician himself suddenly disappeared. There was no reappearance, leaving the audience baffled.

Investigation was made beneath the stage, but no evidence of Victor—or of the pig, the chicken, or the watch—was found. According to police, the stage had no trapdoors or secret compartments corresponding to the location from which the magician apparently vanished.

When questioned, his assistant—a young man by the name of Babu Rabu—claimed to have no knowledge of the whereabouts of Victor. Babu, who was as engaging and pleasant as Victor had been dark and mysterious, promised that he would continue the theatrical engagement through its scheduled conclusion on the seventh day of this month.

It is alleged by one member of the audience—one Miss Starfield, a traveler from Back East—that Babu Rabu had, in fact, pushed his master into the hole in the floor. But other audience members disputed Miss Starfield's story, terming her "fanciful" and "a hysterical female."

Dale looked up and said, "So what's the deal? Okay, so this Babu guy takes over in 1874. Even so, it can't all be the same Victor all those years. The first posters start around 1700. He supposedly disappears in 1874. He'd have to be like two hundred years old by then."

There was no answer. The librarian was no longer sitting at his desk.

"Mr. Dinwiddie?" Dale called. "Mr. Dinwiddie?"

Still no answer. He wandered through the large room, looking behind shelves and racks. But the librarian was gone.

And when Dale came back out to the front of the room, he noticed that the dog was gone, too.

Nervously, Dale cracked open the door and peeked out. No dog.

"Huh," he said. "Weird."

XIX

I'd be careful," Jessica said. "It's a really big, spooky-looking dog."

The clattering got louder and louder. The security guards looked nervous.

And suddenly the dog appeared at the door. When it saw the two security guards, it stopped. It had the book—slightly charred around the edges—clamped firmly in its mouth. Its yellow eyes stared at the first security guard then at the second—like it was considering which one to have for lunch first.

"What kind of dog *is* that?" the younger of the two guards said.

"I don't intend to find out," the other guard said. With that he dropped his keys and sprinted for the front door of the library.

The second guard cleared his throat nervously. "Good boy," he said, his voice high and shaky. He held out his hand. It was trembling. "Just . . . give me the book."

The dog growled and made a sudden movement, like it was about to charge the second security guard.

"Okay, I ain't paid enough for this," the guard said. And he, too, hightailed it toward the front door.

"What are we going to do?" Jessica said.

The director started backing slowly away from the dog. "Just back away slowly," he said softly. "Don't make any sudden moves."

For a moment the big lobby was utterly silent. Then Jessica heard a sharp tapping noise above them. She looked up at the staircase. Coming down the stairs was a tall blond woman wearing black clothes and dark sunglasses. It was the woman who had said her name was Miss Star, the librarian from the Braille Room. She carried a white cane, which she rapped sharply on the marble. But it didn't seem like she needed the cane. She walked with the confidence of someone who could see perfectly.

"Ah, Jessica," she said. "I see you've found my dog."

The director looked up at the blind woman. Then his face went white. "No," he said softly. "Not *her*."

The blind woman kept tapping her cane as she descended the stairs. Everyone seemed to have deserted the area to get away from the giant dog, which was still crouched in the doorway, its teeth bared, hackles raised. The tapping of the cane echoed in the marble hallway.

"You!" the director of the library said again.

The blind woman approached Jessica. She seemed uninterested in the librarian. "Oh, hello again, sweetie," she said to Jessica. Then she snapped her finger at the huge dog, which was still standing in the doorway of the stairwell.

The dog stopped growling and trotted obediently to the woman.

"Oh, silly boy, you've slobbered all over Jess's nice book," the blind woman said. She grabbed the book, and the dog let go of it instantly.

"You're not supposed to be here," the director of the library said.

"Well, obviously I am, though," Miss Star said. Then she turned to Jessica. "Would you like your book back?"

"Yes," Jessica said.

"I'm sorry, but I'm not giving it to you," Miss Star said. "Not yet anyway."

"It's mine," Jessica said.

"Let's go for a drive," she said firmly. "We'll talk." Then she began tapping toward the massive front door of the library, the dog trailing behind here.

"Don't do it!" the library director whispered fearfully. "She's not supposed to be here."

"Who is she?"

"If you want your book back, sweetie, you'll have to come with me," the blind woman said, waving the slightly charred volume in the air.

Jessica hesitated.

The director said, "She's—"

But he didn't finish because the woman interrupted. "Plus, I'll tell you who you really are!"

Jess felt stunned, like she'd just been hit by lightning.

Who she really was? What in the world was the woman talking about?

As Miss Star disappeared through the door, the director tried again. "Don't go, Jessica. She's—"

But it was too late.

Jessica was already bursting out into the sunshine.

XX

Dale walked out of the room and looked tentatively down into the hallway, searching for any sign of the dog. Nothing. It was empty in both directions. He had no idea where Jessica was. No idea whether or not she was safe. He figured he'd try the lobby. That would be the natural place to meet.

He walked to the stairwell, took the stairs up to the lobby, peeked out. The lobby was empty, too. No dog. He walked down and sat on a bench by the door. After ten or fifteen minutes, he started to feel nervous. The entire place seemed abandoned. How odd.

Had there been some kind of evacuation that he hadn't heard about? A bomb scare, a fire drill, something like that?

He decided to head over to Jessica's house and see if she was there.

He was surprised to find a strange car parked in the driveway of Jessica's house. He knocked on the door. After a minute it opened, and a lady Dale didn't know very well was standing there. Mrs. Ellis—wasn't that her name? She had a son named Ben or Bill or something who was in high school.

"Hello," she said, smiling pleasantly.

"Uh . . . hi," he said. "I was looking for Jessica."

She frowned. "Jessica . . . Sternhagen?"

He nodded. "Yeah, sure. She's a friend of mine."

Mrs. Ellis looked very puzzled. "Is there some reason she would—" Mrs. Ellis frowned for a moment. "You know, the strangest thing happened today. She came over here and walked right into our house. Just like she owned it."

Dale felt something twist in his stomach. "Uh . . . well . . . she does, doesn't she?" He paused. "I mean, her parents do."

Mrs. Ellis kept frowning at him. "Her parents sold the house to us, gosh, two years ago maybe?"

Dale's eyes widened slightly. "Oh. I thought . . ."

"They moved down to Rose Lane after"—she lowered her voice—"after what happened to her father."

"Rose Lane?" That was where Dale's house was.

Mrs. Ellis nodded, then sighed. "What a tragedy. I hear he just hasn't been the same since."

"Okay. Sorry to bother you."

Dale turned and fled down the street. Rose Lane? What in the world was going *on* here?

He ran down the block, turned the corner, and cut through Edgewood Creek, a subdivision where a lot of the managers from the pork factory lived. There was a shortcut at the tennis courts that would get him into his own neighborhood.

As he was trotting down Willoughbrook Court, a pleasant voice called: "Hey! There he is!"

It was a man in the front yard of a house, playing touch football with his kids. The man turned toward Dale and passed the ball toward him. "Think quick, champ!"

Instinctively Dale tracked the ball as it flew toward him. There was nothing special about it. All footballs fly the same way. They go up, they come down. And yet, it was like he remembered the exact, precise path of the ball. The high, clean arc of it as it spiraled across the brilliant blue sky. Like he knew where it would be before it even got there. Like he . . . *remembered* it. Which was impossible. Because you couldn't remember the future, could you?

But before making the catch, he snuck a quick peek at the man's face.

And then something strange happened. It was like one of those moments in a movie where the whole world freezes. The man in the yard—he looked exactly like his dad. Except his own father never smiled like that. And didn't have a neat haircut, or wear a golf outfit, or look so . . . handsome and content and in control. So happy.

But deep in his bones, Dale knew it was his father. The happy man was his father.

Which was also impossible.

Plus there was the minor fact that his father couldn't throw footballs. He didn't have a right hand.

It was the strangest thing. All his life Dale had dreamed of this—that one day his dad would come out in the yard and play touch football with Dale and his brothers. That he'd be fun and cool. That he'd pay attention to Dale.

But he'd known it was just a fantasy, that it could never happen for real.

But in that moment he realized that this was no fantasy. It had all come true. Something had happened, something in the past, something that had changed his father into this genial fun guy. A guy with two hands. Dale felt flooded with gratitude and relief.

Wham!

The ball smacked Dale right in the side of the head.

"Oh!" the man who seemed to be Dale's father said. "Oh, that's gotta hurt."

Then he charged toward Dale, grabbed him in a big hug, and said, "You okay, champ?"

"Dad?" Dale said.

"Of course I'm your dad!" His father suddenly looked worried. He squinted at Dale, studying his face. "Boy, that sucker must have hit you harder than I thought. You look a little shook up. Come on inside and lie down for a second!"

He picked Dale up and ran into the house. "Donna? Donna, I just clocked Dale with the football. I think it kinda rang his bell."

Dale's mother ran out from the kitchen. She was wearing an apron. And makeup. And had her hair done. She actually looked kind of pretty. Instead of strained and twitchy and worn-out. It was the most bizarre thing.

And the house? The house his father had run into was nicely decorated and clean. It didn't smell like cigarettes and beer, but like home-baked cookies and detergent.

"Dale!" his mother shouted. "Dale, are you okay?"

Dale lay on the couch, looking up at the ceiling. The entire family crowded around him. Owen and Molly and Rick and Buggy and Crystal and Justin and Allie. He didn't think that ever in his entire life had the entire family looked at him all at once.

"Son?" His father leaned over him, touched him gently on the forehead. Dale noticed his dad was wearing a plastic name tag on his shirt that said:

EDGAR McDUFFIE
• Director of Compliance •

Dale sat up slowly. "I'm fine, Dad," he said. Something was swelling in his chest, swelling so it felt like he might burst open. "I just . . . aren't you supposed to be at work or something?" Dale wasn't sure why, but he knew that his dad—*this* Dad—usually worked all day on Saturday.

His father frowned. "Yeah, well, felt a little fuzzy-headed today, decided to knock off early. Soon as I got home, though, I felt great again."

"I know what you mean," Dale said. "I kinda feel the same way."

"Well, you gave me quite a little scare, I'll tell you that!" Dale's father looked up at his mother, his face getting serious. "It was the spookiest thing. He looked me right in the face, and for a second I swear he didn't know who I was. I about had a heart attack."

Dale's mother sat down beside him on the couch and stroked his face. "Honey? Are you okay."

"I'm fine," he said. He looked around at the circle of faces. "Can we just go out and play some football?"

His father laughed, a relieved expression on his face. "Not now, champ," he said. "You really need to rest for a minute."

Dale lay back down and closed his eyes. Of all the strange things that had happened today, this seemed like the strangest. Giant dogs and stuff—that he could handle. But parents who noticed him? And seemed to care about him? He just couldn't fathom it. He felt flooded with happiness.

"Dale? Dale?" It was his mother again.

He opened his eyes. She was still there, the pretty mother with the apron and her hair done.

"Did you just faint?" she said.

Dale smiled. Suddenly his vision got all blurry, like he had tears welling up in his eyes. He wiped them quickly so that nobody would see. "No! No, I'm fine. I'm totally fine."

After a few minutes everybody drifted away, leaving Dale sitting on the couch by himself. He looked around.

The house was so *nice*! He couldn't believe it. It wasn't like it was fancy or anything. But it was clean. There were pictures hanging on the walls, a bookshelf with an encyclopedia and a few paperbacks standing over by the far wall, a nice carpet on the floor, chairs that matched the couch. The same as in all those fantasies he'd had all these years.

How did this happen?

Or maybe, another way of looking at it, why had things gone so bad in his real life? And what if this *was* his real life? Maybe the other life he'd been living had been some kind of sham, some kind of mistake. Maybe this *was* what it was supposed to be like.

All these questions were zooming around in his head at high speed. And he had nobody to talk to about them. He wished that Jessica were here.

His father came into the room, turned on the news. The newscaster was talking about a war in Bulgaria. *Bulgaria? Huh? There was no war in—*

Dale's father shook his head sadly. "Boy, would you look at that, Dale? Another two hundred casualties over there. Tragic." He reached over and put his arm around Dale's shoulders, almost like he wanted to protect him from harm.

Suddenly Dale started feeling like his head was hurting. He needed to find Jessica, big-time. This was all too bizarre. There wasn't supposed to be a war in Bulgaria.

"I gotta go, Dad," he said.

"Be back by six-thirty," his father said. "We've got that father-son banquet thing at the church, remember?"

Church? Dale thought as he ran out the door. Father-son banquet? Last he'd heard, Dale's father hadn't been in a church in thirty years. And certainly not with Dale. This was getting weirder and weirder.

XXI

Two minutes after they left the library, Jessica and Miss Star, the woman with the long blond hair and the white cane, were zooming down the road in a sporty red German car, with the top down and electronic dance music blasting on the stereo. Miss Star's long blond hair was streaming in the wind. She looked extremely glamorous with her high cheekbones and her dark sunglasses. The big scary dog, Cerberus, was sitting in the back, its head sticking out where the window would have been if the top hadn't been down already.

"So I guess you're not really blind?" Jessica said. "Since you're driving and all."

The woman turned down the music. "Blind? That's a matter of opinion."

"You're either blind or you're not," Jessica said firmly. "Now give me my book back."

"Most of the people you know," the woman who was probably not blind said, "their eyes work just fine. But do they actually *see* much of anything?"

"That's different," Jessica said. "That's metaphorical."

She scowled. "Now give me my book." The book was sitting in the woman's lap. Jessica made a grab for it.

"Oop! Hup! Nope!" Miss Star said, sliding the book just out of Jessica's grasp. In the backseat the dog growled menacingly. Jessica felt the dog's breath on her neck. It was making her nervous. "I'll give you the book later."

"Why not now? It's mine."

"Because you and I need to get some things sorted out."

Jessica was feeling irritated. "Hold on, hold on. Who are you really? I assume you're not really Miss—"

"Star? It's as good a name as any. You don't have to call me Miss, though. Just Star."

"Okay, Star."

"But let's not talk about me. Let's talk about you."

"What about me?"

Star had reached the outskirts of town and was now heading out on U.S. 10, the highway that headed down toward St. Cloud. There were farms on both sides of the road, and they were whizzing by at a very high rate of speed. Star kept pushing the accelerator until they were going over a hundred miles an hour. Jessica wished she would slow down.

"So," Star said. "Big day for you, huh?"

Jessica shrugged. "How did you know?"

The woman looked at her and gave her a funny smile, like they were sharing some kind of secret. "Your big destiny and all that stuff? Wow. Who'da thunk it?"

Jessica glared at Star. "First, you're going too fast and you're scaring me. Second—"

"Second, in the back of your mind, you think it's all a bunch of bull, right? Destiny, saving the world, blah blah blah?"

Jessica shrugged. "I don't know."

Suddenly Star stomped on the brakes, and the car slowed with a screech. Cerberus was thrown forward, his head resting for a moment on Jessica's shoulder. Jessica was surprised to find the sensation kind of pleasant. For some reason she didn't find the dog frightening at all anymore.

Star turned off the road onto a small gravel track that led to a chain-link fence.

"We'll have to walk from here," Star said, hopping out of the car and flipping open her folded white cane. Cerberus leaped out of the car onto the ground.

Jessica followed Star, the big dog running ahead of them, as though it knew exactly where they were going. They passed a small sign on the fence that said:

Absurdly dangerous abandoned rock quarry!!!
DO NOT ENTER!!!!!!!
This means you, you complete moron!!!!!!!!!!!!!!!!!

Star walked briskly past the sign, tapping away with the white cane. She was still carrying *Her Lif* in the other hand. "Does it seem fair?" she said to Jessica. Jessica didn't understand why she was bothering with the cane charade. "Does it seem fair that all this saving-the-world stuff should get dumped on an eleven-year-old girl?"

Jessica hadn't really thought about it. Or . . . well, maybe it had been in the back of her mind. But she hadn't thought about it much. "I don't know."

"Because I don't think it's fair." Star was walking down a footpath into the woods now, pushing through the brush with her long legs, the cane probing in front of her like a long white finger. Jessica had to struggle to keep up. "I mean, they tell you, 'Oh, congratulations, you're going to save the world! Yay for you!' But they don't tell you what it's going to cost you."

"What do you mean?"

Star didn't answer. After a minute they came out of the woods and found themselves at the edge of a high cliff. Below them was a small pond or lake, impossibly blue, its walls formed by the sheer rock of the abandoned quarry. Star stood right at the edge, her cane hanging off into empty space. It made Jessica a little nervous.

"What do you mean, cost?" Jessica pursued.

Star turned and looked at Jessica. For the first time she took off her sunglasses. Her eyes were a strange pale blue. And they had no pupils. She smiled thinly at Jessica.

Jessica felt a knot in her stomach. The woman hadn't been kidding! "You really *are* blind? How do you drive?"

Star ignored her question. "Saving the world," she said. "It's not really as dramatic as they make it out to be. The truth is, there are a lot of different worlds, a lot of possible universes. Every time we make a choice, we make a new world. I grant you, sure, some worlds are better than others. What they want you to do is to choose one particular world. Infinite possibilities floating around out there, and they want you to just . . . snatch one of them out of the air!"

"They told me there's a true and correct universe, a—"

"They gave you the road story, right? The universe is like a giant road, right? It's a road going back into infinity and it's splitting all the time and you have to save the main road so that the whole thing doesn't get dragged off and thrown out of whack and blah blah blah."

"That's what the library director said, yeah."

Star squinted at her skeptically. "Well, frankly, that's a controversial theory. Some people don't even think it's true." She blew a bunch of air out of her cheeks and rolled her unseeing eyes. "*Saving* the world? No, not really. Even the nicest worlds have a lot of pain and nastiness in them. And the worst worlds, they have light and goodness in them. So . . . no, if I were you, I wouldn't do it. I'd refuse. Just go back and live your life and let somebody else worry about the fate of the universe."

Jessica glared at her. The more she knew the woman, the less she liked her. And she hadn't liked her *that* much to begin with. "There's a big difference between having some crummy stuff happen . . . and having the whole thing go *poof* and disappearing."

The woman's sightless blue eyes stared out over the still pond. "I don't really think it'll come to that."

The big dog came up to Jessica, sniffed her up and down, its wet muzzle probing and poking at her. Then, suddenly, Cerberus turned and darted off into the trees.

"Give me the book," Jessica said.

The woman looked a little sad for a minute. "You have no idea of the sacrifices you're in for."

Jessica felt something welling up inside of her. Not just anger, but a sense that if she didn't move quickly, something really bad was about to happen. "Give. Me. My. Book."

"Well, I thought it was only fair to show you what I'm about to do."

"Give me—"

Jessica made another grab for the book. But she was too late. The blind woman suddenly cocked her arm and hurled the book into the air. It flew in a high arc through the clear blue sky, the pages riffling and flapping in the air.

"Wait!" Jessica shouted. "That's my *book*! That's my *life*!"

"Not anymore."

The book hit the water with a splat. For a moment it just sat there, floating placidly on the water.

"Hey!" Jessica shouted. "What is *wrong* with you, you . . . you . . . you . . . butt face!"

"Trust me," Star said with a sad smile. "I just saved you a lot of grief."

"I'm *fine*," Jessica said. "I *want* to do something cool. I *want* to save the universe. I *want* to be more than just some skinny weird girl living in some boring town where nothing ever happens. It's not your decision."

"Oh, but it is. More than you know."

"What's that supposed to mean?"

Star put her sunglasses back on, covering her strange and sightless eyes. "Has it sunk yet, Jess?"

Jessica looked out at the water but didn't answer. She was hopping mad. She wanted to jump in and try to swim out toward the book before it sank. But the water was just so far down. And Jessica was scared of heights. What if she got hurt in the fall? A ring of tiny waves was slowly making its way toward the edges of the still pond.

"Why does everybody keep talking about saving me from grief and heartache and all this junk?" Jessica said angrily. "It's *my* life."

Star turned sharply toward her. "*Who* was talking to you about grief and heartache?" she demanded.

"Just some guy. He came to my house and tried to sell my mom this creepy vacuum cleaner."

Star's face suddenly turned white. "Wait a minute! What was his name?"

Jessica shrugged, then looked back down into the pond. The book was slowly sinking beneath the blue surface of the water. "I forget. Bob Something, Junior. Robbins, maybe?"

Star sucked in her breath sharply. "Oh no," she said softly. "Not Babu . . ."

Jessica kept watching the book. Suddenly it disappeared

beneath the surface of the water. A large bubble rose to the surface. *Bloop.* And then the book was gone.

"Oh, no," Star repeated. "I've made a terrible—"

Jessica turned back to see what Star was talking about.

But to her amazement—the woman was gone.

Not gone like hiding behind a tree. *Gone,* gone.

"Star?" Jessica called.

Nothing.

Which was when it occurred to her—Star had said she was going to tell her the truth about her life. But she'd never had the chance.

Jessica stared out at the water, an empty feeling in the pit of her stomach.

Dale was feeling really discombobulated. After leaving the library, he had hiked over to Jessica's house. Only, it wasn't her house anymore. The Ellises lived there. When he had asked Mrs. Ellis if she knew where Jessica was, she had given him the strangest look, and then said that the Stern-hagens had moved to Rose Lane a few years ago.

Rose Lane. The street Dale had lived on before. So, Dale had walked over to Rose Lane and walked up and down the street, trying to figure out where Jessica's house was. It was strange, the small differences. One of the houses was just gone—the one where that mean guy lived, Mr. Lewis, with the crazy pit bull.

Across the street was his own house. Only it wasn't his own house anymore. Not in this universe anyway. He stared at it for a while. Something about it made him feel queasy.

Then he heard a slow, rhythmic thumping coming from the back of the house. He decided to see what it was. He walked down the weedy driveway, which led around the side to a freestanding garage in the corner of the small backyard.

He found Jessica's father.

Or at least he *seemed* to be Jessica's father. He had the same face. But something was different. There was a funny scar right at his hairline. Had that been there before? Dale wasn't sure. He looked bitter and tired, too—like a tube of Crest with all the toothpaste squeezed out of it. Mr. Sternhagen was seated on a folding beach chair, throwing a ratty green tennis ball at the side of the garage. Throwing, catching, throwing, catching. An old radio sat on the ground next to him, playing a broadcast of a Twins game.

Mr. Sternhagen looked up at Dale. "Oh. Hi, Dale," he said. He didn't smile, and his voice was an uncharacteristic monotone.

"Is Jessica here?"

Mr. Sternhagen shrugged. "Haven't seen her in a while." He kept throwing the ball against the wall of the garage. There was a large spot on the wall where all the paint was gone. He must have thrown it at the wall an awful lot of times to knock all that paint off. "Doctor said it was good for me, throwing the ball. Helps my coordination."

"Your coordination? Is something wrong with your co-ordination?"

Mr. Sternhagen looked at him curiously. "You know," he said. "From the accident."

"Oh." Dale didn't know what to say. He didn't know what accident Mr. Sternhagen was talking about.

The announcer on the radio said the Twins were down three–zip in the bottom of the third. Mr. Sternhagen threw the ball a couple more times. *Thump. Thump. Thump.*

"Funny," Mr. Sternhagen said, "I think about it every day. Usually I have dessert at lunch. But the day of the accident, I skipped dessert. For my health, you know? Thought I was doing the smart thing. But if I'd just stayed in the lunchroom for the time it takes to eat a Twinkie? I wouldn't have been there when the machine went haywire. I'd still be healthy as a horse. We'd still be living back on Grant Street."

"Huh," Dale said.

Thump. Thump.

"One little choice," said Mr. Sternhagen. "You make one tiny little choice. And that's it. No going back. No fixing it. There's no ERASE button in life, kid. No ERASE button."

Suddenly tears were rolling down Mr. Sternhagen's face. Dale had never felt so uncomfortable in his entire life. Grown men weren't supposed to cry.

"Sorry," Mr. Sternhagen said. "The accident. They say it affected the part of my brain that controls—" He sighed, pointed at his face, the two streams of tears running down the sides of his nose. "I can't do a thing about it." He wiped his eyes with the ratty tennis ball, then started throwing the ball at the wall again. It was almost like he'd forgotten Dale was standing there.

Dale felt a rising sadness. But not just sadness. It was like he was feeling two different emotions at the same time. Because—stronger than the sadness—he also felt . . . what?—something completely opposite from what he was supposed to feel. It took him a minute to realize what it was. He was happy. He was glad. Whatever had changed in the universe, it had made things better for him. Dale felt a strange wave of selfish pleasure.

"What if you could?" Dale said.

"What if I could what?" Mr. Sternhagen said.

"Hit the ERASE button. Go back and change it."

Mr. Sternhagen looked at him like he was an idiot. "I'd go back and eat the freakin' Twinkie, kid. Are you stupid?"

Something struck Dale now. "Okay, but like what if you knew that if you ate the Twinkie you'd be fine. But also . . . let's say . . . what if when the machine went haywire, it would kill somebody else. And that person, if he'd lived, would have had a kid. And that kid would have grown up and discovered a cure for cancer. What would you do then?"

Mr. Sternhagen threw the ball at the wall a little harder. "I'd eat the freakin' Twinkie," he said harshly.

"Even if the machine was—"

"I heard what you said!" Mr. Sternhagen shouted. "I'd eat the Twinkie! I don't care who it hurt. I don't care about all the people with cancer. Look at me! That machine went haywire, and look at me now!" He stood up from the chair and staggered toward Dale. There was something bad wrong with him. Something about the way he walked. It seemed like he had to make a special effort to pick up his left foot, and then at each step it flopped down on the ground like a wet mop. There was something monstrous about it. Something creepy and horrible and sad.

"Get out of here, kid!" Jessica's father shouted, throwing the tennis ball at Dale. "I'm sick of your questions. You're as bad as Jessica! *Why, why, why?* Always a question. I'm sick of hearing it!"

Dale dodged out of the way of the ball. He'd never heard Mr. Sternhagen say anything like that before in his life. He'd always been the nicest guy in the world. A little boring, maybe. But major-league nice.

"Get outta here!"

Dale didn't have to be told again. He ran out of the backyard and into the street, his pulse thundering in his ears.

XXII

Dun-dun-dun-DUUUUUUUHHHHHHHHH!" Jessica
heard a voice behind her. But it wasn't Star. Star was
completely and utterly gone. It was a man's voice.

She turned and saw the vacuum cleaner guy, Bob Robbins Jr., standing behind her.

"Pretty cool, huh?" he said. "Just disappearing into thin
air like that?"

Jessica stared at him.

"Yeah, I know, I know. Seems crazy, huh? Violation of
the laws of physics and all that? Was that your first CI?"

"CI?"

"Chronological infarction."

"My first *what*?"

"Chronological infarction. That is the term describing
an event in which a person, place, thing, or event is ren-
dered nonpossible based on a temporal feedback loop in
which the occlusion of . . . well . . ." He shrugged. "It gets
kinda technical, the explanation. Bottom line, that lady you
were talking to? Somebody did something that made it so
that she never existed anymore."

"That doesn't make sense," Jessica said. "Nonpossible? It's not even correct grammar. 'Never existed anymore?' You can't put those words in the same sentence like that."

Bob Robbins Jr. grinned. "Hey, I just did."

She looked at him for a minute. He had a point. And probably when a person disappears in front of your eyes, grammar is not the main thing you should be worrying about.

"Want a ride?" Bob Robbins Jr. said.

"I want my—" Jessica was going to say that she wanted her book back. But then she thought, *Hey, maybe it would be better not to mention the book.* The book hadn't dematerialized. It was just underwater. There had to be some way of getting it out. If she left with Bob Robbins Jr. then at least she would know that he wasn't here fishing the book out of the water. It occurred to her that the coach of the girls' basketball team, Coach Slocum, was always talking about how he went scuba diving every summer down in Jamaica. Maybe if—

"Hey!" Bob Robbins Jr. waved his hands in front of Jessica's face. "Earth to Jessica. When that lady disappeared, her nice car disappeared, too. If you want to get back to town in time for dinner, you'll need to hitch a ride with somebody."

Jessica quickly came to a decision. She didn't trust the guy at all. She didn't want to ride with him. But right now she was low on options. If she wanted to get the scuba gear and come back to get the book, she'd have to go with him. "Okay," she said. "Let's go."

"Hey!" he called after her. "You got the book, right? My information tells me you are now supposed to have the book in your hot little hand."

She didn't answer him, just kept walking faster. So apparently he hadn't gotten there in time to see Star throw the book into the water. That was a good thing.

It was only as she came out of the woods that the whole thing struck her. She was supposed to have gotten the book. And she'd failed. At the very least, if she didn't get it back she was going to be stuck in this universe, where her family was unhappy and her dad's brain was scrambled and—

Suddenly her legs felt weak and her head felt funny. Next thing she knew, she was sitting on a stump with her head between her legs.

"You okay?" Bob Robbins Jr. said. "You look a little pooped."

Jessica took several deep breaths. Then she stood up and walked toward the white van parked by the road.

"I'm fine," she said.

"Good," he said, "because there's an extremely large dog over there. And it looks like it wouldn't mind eating you. If I were you, I think I'd probably start running."

XXIII

Jessica turned and saw the dog. Cerberus was back in the trees, maybe thirty yards away. Just a couple of minutes ago—while Star was still there—he had seemed perfectly nice, perfectly tame. But now? Now he looked ready to bite somebody in half. The dog's long teeth were bared, and a string of drool hung from its jowls. A deep growl welled up from its chest. Her heart began beating wildly.

"Me?" Bob Robbins added. "Not a big fan of dogs."

Then he was off like a shot, running toward the van—which was parked on the side of the highway about a hundred yards away.

Jessica didn't think. She just started running, too. The dog came after them. She could hear its footfalls thumping after her. They sounded impossibly heavy, like somebody was dropping a bunch of huge weights on the ground behind her.

But she didn't dare look over her shoulder.

It seemed like the van was a million miles away now. And the dog's heavy tread was getting closer and closer.

But then, just as the dog drew up near her, she was shocked to see it blaze past her like it didn't even notice her.

Next thing she knew, the dog had reached the van. Bob Robbins Jr.—his hand fumbling with the door handle—turned with a look of panic on his face. He froze.

"Good dog," he said in a high, nervous voice. "Easy there!"

The dog stood in front of him, hackles raised like needles on its shoulders, eyes pinned on Bob Robbins, growling slightly. Bob Robbins Jr. looked frozen, his hand on the door handle.

"Uh . . . little help here, somebody?" Bob Robbins said. He knocked gently on the glass, obviously hoping that his henchman inside the van would help him. The man inside the van showed no particular interest in getting out of the van, however.

For a moment Jessica thought she might just run on by the van, keep running and running until she could flag down a car. Leave Bob Robbins Jr. to fend for himself.

But for reasons she didn't really understand, she came to a halt, not ten feet from the van. And the dog.

Suddenly a picture popped into her mind—almost like a memory—of her standing next to the huge dog, holding it on a leash, walking it, feeding it. *How strange,* she thought. *Cerberus is not my dog.* But in that moment, her fear of the dog completely dropped away.

"Cerberus!" she said firmly. "Sit."

The dog sniffed the air for a moment, looked over at

her, cocked its head like it was slightly confused about something. Then it sat meekly. Its hackles went down. But it continued to stare fixedly at Bob Robbins Jr.

"Lie down!" Bob Robbins said. The dog growled at him, bared its teeth a little. Its hackles went up again.

"Lie down," Jessica said. The dog lay down.

She felt an odd confidence rising inside. Bob Robbins Jr. looked at her and frowned curiously. "Well, now *this* is a fascinating turn of events, huh?" he said.

"You can open the door now," Jessica said. "He won't hurt you."

"And you know this . . . *how?*"

"I just do," Jessica said. And she did. She wasn't sure why, but she knew.

Bob Robbins hastily jumped into the front seat of the van. Jessica tugged open the back door of the van. "In!" she said.

The dog hopped up and jumped into the van.

"Whooooa!" Bob Robbins Jr. said, shrinking away from the huge dog. "Not in the van."

"You want me to come with you?" she said. "Or not?"

Bob Robbins Jr. cleared his throat. "Okay," he said. "But you better keep that dog under control."

Jessica jumped in and sat down. "Sit, Cerberus!" she said. The big dog lay on the floor at her feet. She reached down and stroked its fur. Which was surprisingly soft.

"For a guy who plans to be master of the universe or whatever," she said, "you're kind of a scaredy-cat."

Bob Robbins Jr. turned and looked at her through narrowed eyes. "I'm starting to not like you so much," he said.

She smiled at him. "That's okay. I *never* liked you."

For the first time she saw something nervous in Bob Robbins's eyes. Up until the dog had started chasing him, he had seemed supremely confident. But now . . . now he seemed to be losing his spirit.

Was it the dog that was making her suddenly feel so confident? She wasn't sure. All she knew was that something just felt right at that moment.

"Good boy," she said to Cerberus. "Good dog!"

The dog put its head on its paws and closed its eyes.

Suddenly Bob Robbins looked happy again. "So," he said as they drove into downtown Alsberg, "what's the plan, kiddo?"

Jessica waited until they pulled up at the stoplight in front of Jaarvik's Drugstore. Jessica quickly yanked the door handle open. "The plan is, *See ya later!*" She jumped out. The dog bounded out after her.

"Hey, whoa, wait a sec!" Bob Robbins Jr. called. "You're not going anywhere."

"Cerberus," Jessica said. "Guard!"

The dog turned and growled at Bob Robbins Jr.

"Okay, okay," Bob Robbins said, "you don't need to get all belligerent on me. I can see when my peculiar talents and abilities are not sufficiently appreciated." He pointed his finger at her. "Five o'clock. I want that book." Then he turned to his henchman. "Let's roll, Dingle."

The light changed, and the van pulled smoothly away, heading toward the west side of town. Jessica watched them until they were gone, then she petted the dog. It rubbed its head against her arm, like it had known her all its life.

Which was very peculiar. Because obviously it hadn't.

"Okay," Jessica said to the dog. "Let's go find some scuba gear."

XXIV

The house smelled of cookies when Dale got home. Home. It was hard to think of this beautiful house as his real home. But it was . . . right?

Once in a blue moon his mom would make those cookies that came in a plastic tube. She never made cookies from scratch. But today when he walked into the kitchen, there she was, stirring a batch of dough in a bowl, flour dusting her hands. "Don't you touch those cookies," she said sharply. "These are for the church fund-raiser tomorrow." Then she smiled mischievously. "Well, maybe you could take one or two."

She poured him a glass of milk, then watched him as he ate a chocolate chip cookie. He could feel the chocolate melting in his mouth as he ate. It seemed like the best cookie he'd ever had in his life. His mother kept watching him.

"What?" he said.

His mother shrugged. "I don't know. I was just feeling lucky for minute. I have such a nice family. Such great kids. It's a great life we have."

Dale swallowed. "You ever think that it might have turned out differently?" he said.

She looked thoughtfully out the window. "That's what I mean," she said. She started spooning blobs of dough onto a cookie sheet. "I just had the strongest feeling. I can't explain it exactly. But I had this sudden feeling, like my life could have easily taken another path."

"I know exactly what you mean," Dale said.

His mother gave him a long, probing look. Then she went back to putting cookie dough on the cookie sheet. "There was a time back when you were in kindergarten when your father got hurt down at the plant. He couldn't work for a while. Money got tight. He started sitting around feeling sorry for himself. I got depressed. You probably don't even remember it." She smiled sadly. "Anyway, one day we got the strangest phone call. This person told us that an appointment had been made for your dad down at the Mayo Clinic in Rochester. Top hand surgeon in the world. We went down there, and this nice surgeon, Dr. Kling, he fixed your father's hand. Your father went back to work. Everything was fine." She took a long slow breath. "But what if that call had never come?"

Dale stared at her.

"I just had . . . it was like a picture in my mind," his mother said. She shivered slightly. "It was such an intense thing. Suddenly I saw myself living another life. Your father was lazing around the house, drinking beer and snapping at everybody. I was feeling sorry for myself. Bills were piling up. No food in the fridge. And we were still living in that miserable little shack we rented over on Rose Lane the year after we got married." She laughed suddenly and waved the back of her hand in the air. "Of course, it's crazy. That never would have happened. We're not the kind of people who'd live like that for long."

"How do you know that?" Dale said.

His mother's smile faded. "Don't talk like that," she said, her eyes going hard for a moment. "Just be grateful for what you have."

Dale looked around, feeling a rush of gratitude and pleasure. "Oh, I am," he said. "Believe me." Then the doorbell rang. "I'll get it," he said.

Dale walked to the door, threw it open. Jessica stood on the front porch.

And for some reason his heart sank. And it wasn't just because of the huge yellow-eyed dog standing meekly behind her.

"Hey," she said. "You're never gonna guess what just happened."

Dale just stared at her.

"You gonna invite me in?" she said. "Or what?"

"How'd you find me?"

"The phone book."

He looked over her shoulder. "What about the dog?" he said.

She grinned. "Oh, don't worry about him." She pointed at a spot in the yard. "Stay, Cerberus!" The dog trotted obligingly to the spot she was pointing at, then lay down. "He won't move."

Dale had been looking for her for the past hour or two. But now that she'd found him, he halfway wished she hadn't. *What was up with that?* he wondered.

She pushed the door open and brushed past him. "Wow!" she said, looking around. "Big change, huh?"

Dale nodded.

"So," she said. "You know where I can get some scuba gear?"

"Why?" Dale said. He had this dull knot in his stomach. He wished she would just go away.

Jessica seemed oblivious to his feelings, though. "I know where the book is. This lady I met at the library threw it into the water out at that old quarry on the Saint Cloud highway. I can get it. But I need some scuba gear."

"Scuba gear." What in the world was she thinking? She didn't know squat about scuba diving. Plus, now that he thought about it, he wasn't sure he wanted to find that book. Frankly, he'd be happy if he could just stay right here.

"It's pretty deep water. We'll need—" Jessica broke off for a moment. For the first time she seemed to really notice him. She peered at him like he was some kind of science experiment. "You seem kinda . . . weird," she said finally. "You okay?"

He looked around. His brothers Rick and Justin ran through the room, laughing, and pounded up the stairs.

It suddenly struck him that he wasn't sure why he and Jessica were friends. Had their friendship just been built on the fact that they were both oddballs, that neither of them fit in? Well, suddenly he was feeling like he fit in a lot better than he used to. And he felt himself noticing how goofy her clothes were—the funny skirt, the high-top sneakers, the odd collection of plastic necklaces she wore around her neck. . . . And how come she never seemed to comb her hair?

"All my life," he said, "I slept in the closet under the stairs. Me and Justin both. Never had a real bed. Kept my clothes in a cardboard box. I couldn't even stretch out all the way without banging into the walls. Never had a real room. Much less a room to myself."

Jessica was watching him intently now.

"I haven't been upstairs in this house yet," he said. "But I know there's a room up there just for me. It's got a bed, blue sheets with footballs printed on them. A chest of drawers full of nice clothes. A little stereo. A football. Posters on the wall. A model of the Red Baron's airplane hanging from the ceiling. I never had any of that stuff."

"So?"

"But that's not the main thing." He took a long, deep breath, sucking in the smell of the cookies. "Look—everybody in this house is happy. My dad plays football in the *yard* with us, Jess!"

Jessica looked at her watch. "Dale, we really need that scuba gear."

"*You* need it."

Jessica squinted at him. "What is your problem, Dale? Seriously. We don't have much time."

"We? Or *you?*"

Jessica looked puzzled. "Huh?"

Dale swallowed. He felt the lump in his stomach grow harder, darker, bigger, colder. And then in a sudden rush, it all came clear to him.

"Jessica," he said softly. "I'm not helping you."

Her eyes widened. "What are you talking about?"

He shook his head. "I can't. If you find that book and go do . . . whatever it is that you're supposed to do with it—it's gonna change things again. It'll change everything back. You'll get your nice house and your nice family back. But me, I'll lose every—" He couldn't even bring himself to say it.

Jessica rubbed her hands across her face, then looked around the room. "Dale," she said finally, "I know this is nice. It's nice not to have to sleep under the stairs anymore. But this place . . . this family . . . this whole world—it's not real."

"It *is!*" Dale rapped on the spotless coffee table with his hand. "It's totally real. And it's better than the world we were in before."

Jessica shook her head.

He grabbed her arm. "You remember that conversation

we had back in fifth grade? What if this is it? What if you drew back the curtain and *this* was the *real* world!"

"I don't think so," she said. "In this world, something bad is happening. Something real bad. I can feel it."

Dale felt prickles run across his skin. "No!"

"Dale—"

"No!" And then Dale felt angry. Angry like he couldn't remember feeling in his whole life. Angry for all the times people had made fun of his cheap clothes. Angry for all the times his father had ignored him. Angry for all the fights and yelling and sadness that had happened in the other house in the other world where he used to live. "No! This *is* the real world!" He slapped his hand on the table so hard it stung. "See? Real wood."

"Dale . . ."

He walked over to the bookshelf and started throwing books onto the floor. "See? Real books!"

Jessica crossed her arms and looked at him like you'd look at any dumb kid having a pointless tantrum. Like she had some kind of secret knowledge that he'd never be privy to.

He grabbed the football off the couch, threw it at the front window. The window shattered as the football burst through it into the front yard. Dale was shouting now. "See? See! Real glass. It's all real!"

Jessica's eyes were wide now.

Dale's mother came into the room. "Dale! What on earth—"

"I'm not going back!" Dale shouted. "I don't care about saving the universe and all that crap! I'm not going!" Dale turned to his mother. "She broke the window! Make her go away!"

Dale's mother looked at Jessica and frowned. "Jess, I don't know what's going on here. But I think you had better leave."

"But I didn't do it! I just came to get Dale's help. I need him to—"

"Please." Dale's mother pointed at the door. "Out, Jess. Now."

Jessica's eyes shifted back toward Dale. Dale clamped his mouth shut and glared at her. She stared back at him, betrayal and shock in her eyes. Then, her face went blank. She wheeled around and walked briskly out the door.

As she disappeared from sight, Dale felt like he was going to puke. *What had he just done?*

"I haven't wanted to say it," his mother said, "but that girl is not a good influence on you. That worthless, shiftless family of hers—" She broke off and just shook her head sadly.

Dale ran up the stairs. Without having to think, he knew which room was his. He flung open the door and hurled himself onto his bed. It was all there, just like he'd told Jessica. The bed with the football sheets, the 1-to-48-scale Fokker triplane hanging from the ceiling, the brand-new football lying on the floor.

He buried his face in the pillow and started to cry.

Then—after a few minutes of feeling miserable—the

strangest thing happened. He felt his old life fading in his mind. The memories started growing dimmer and dimmer. After a little while, it was like he was looking at an album of old photographs from somebody else's life. And then even that started to fade.

XXV

Jessica was shaking as she walked away from Dale's new house. She couldn't believe it. She and Dale had been best friends for about as long as she could remember. And in all that time they'd barely ever had a disagreement—much less a flat-out fight like this.

She just didn't understand it. What was he *thinking*? The fate of the world was hanging in the balance here. And he was making a big deal about whether he had his own room or not? It was beneath him.

As she was walking down the street, she saw two police cars zoom by, sirens blaring. They were heading in the direction of the sausage factory. She took the shortcut that came out behind the sausage factory. As she approached the fence behind the sausage factory property, she found a knot of people staring through the fence at something.

"What's going on?" she said to no one in particular.

A dumpy woman with curlers in her hair pointed at the factory, then said, "Look."

Jessica shaded her eyes with her hand. Then she saw it. In the back of the sausage factory was what looked like a large hole in the wall. An inky black hole. No, that wasn't dark enough to describe it. The hole (or whatever it was) was darker than ink—darker and blacker than anything she'd ever seen before. Like it was sucking all the light right out of the air. Workers from the sausage factory, wearing their white coats and hairnets, stood around staring at it.

What was strange was that it wasn't quite like a hole either. It was more of a sphere. But not a solid sphere. You couldn't see through it into the factory. It was just an empty globe of darkness. Nothing going in, nothing coming out. No light, no warmth, no nothing.

And it was getting bigger. Not quickly, but inexorably, unstoppably. Jessica couldn't actually see it getting bigger. But she could feel it. It made her bones hurt, just looking at it.

The police hopped out of their cars over by the factory and started pushing the white-coated workers back and talking furiously on their radios and waving their arms. The police looked all busy and official. But Jessica got the sense they didn't have a clue what to do about the big black thing.

"Well, somebody will know what to do." The dumpy woman with curlers in her hair didn't seem worried. "Maybe the governor'll send an expert."

"I don't know," another woman said. She had a pinched, worried face. "I've never seen anything like it."

"Maybe it's like an alien spacecraft," a kid with thick glasses said. He was carrying a Darth Vader action figure in his hand.

"I think it's gonna eat the sausage factory," another boy said.

"Maybe the aliens like sausage," the kid with Darth Vader said.

"There's no such thing as aliens, dumb head," the other boy said.

"Are too!"

"Are not!"

"Shut up, both of you," the nervous woman said. "You want me to tell your father you were fighting again?"

Jessica took one last look at the strange black thing and then hurried away. She had to get moving! How soon before that black thing did . . . well . . . whatever it was going to do? She didn't know what it was. But she was quite sure it had something to do with whatever Bob Robbins was up to.

Scuba gear. She had to get over to Coach Slocum's as soon as possible. "Come on, Cerberus," she said. She started running down the street. The massive dog loped along behind her.

She reached Coach Slocum's, just a little out of breath, about ten minutes later. She knocked on the door. The coach opened it and looked at her curiously for a moment. Then he smiled.

Coach Slocum was a tall man with very large forearms, pants that were one size too tight, and thinning hair. Well . . . he'd had thinning hair the last time she'd seen him. But today he had a big, thick head of hair that looked suspiciously like it was made out of plastic.

"Well my goodness!" he said. "Look what the cat drug in." Coach Slocum was from somewhere down south and loved using colorful expressions.

"Look, coach," she said, her eyes fixing on his fake-looking hair, "I know this is going to sound weird, but last year in PE class you were talking about how you liked scuba diving, right?"

The coach continued to smile at her. He didn't speak, though.

"So . . . anyway, I kinda need to borrow your scuba diving stuff."

"*Borrow* it? My scuba gear?" He started to laugh.

"It's really, really important," she said.

He scratched his hair. It made a loud scratchy sound. *Plastic*, she thought. *Definitely* plastic. "Hon, I don't know where you got the idea I ever went scuba diving, but . . ." He shrugged. "It just ain't so."

"But . . ." She felt panic rising in her gut. "But last year you told us how you went to Aruba or Barbados or someplace. And how you went scuba diving . . ." The sentence died away in the air. There was no sign of recognition on his face.

Finally he leaned forward and said, "I know you kids joke about my hairpiece," he said. "Don't tell me you don't."

"Uh . . ." she said.

"On the commercials, they say how, oh yeah, you can

wear it in the ocean and all that? Well, fact of the matter is, you get all these shells and stuff stuck in there, you never get 'em out. I always *wanted* to scuba dive. But I just can't. Not with this hairpiece."

Jessica stared at him. "You really don't own any scuba gear?"

"Scout's honor." He gave her his usual smarmy grin, then looked up and down her body, appraising her like she was a pair of pliers he was thinking about buying at Sears. "So, you gonna come out for basketball next fall? You musta grew two, three inches last year."

The thought of playing basketball had zero appeal to Jessica. Running up and down a court trying to put a ball through a metal hoop? The whole thing just seemed so pointless.

"Caitlin Murphy'll be all-conference at point guard this year almost for sure," Coach Slocum said. "Problem is, we got no verticality down in the paint."

Verticality in the paint? Jessica had no idea what he was talking about.

"I'm serious as a heart attack," he said. "You got speed, agility, coordination. I been watching you. If we had a tall girl? Like you? We'd have a shot at the state tournament."

So that's what he meant. Why would somebody say "we need verticality in the paint" when what he really meant was "we want a tall girl"? She was about to make this exact point. But then she thought about it. Maybe there was another way to play this. "Tell you what, coach," she said. "If you find me some scuba gear in the next hour—then I'll play basketball for you."

He winked at her. "Come inside, doll," he said. "I'm owna make a couple phone calls."

Something occurred to Jessica. There were some questions she needed answered before she got her hands on the book again. She looked at her watch. It was past three o'clock. She didn't even have three hours.

"You get the scuba gear, coach. I'll meet you back here in half an hour."

"Hon, you ought to put that dog on a leash," he said, nodding at Cerberus. "I'm a dog lover, sure enough. But that sucker flat out makes me nervous."

Jessica turned and ran down the street again, thinking about her fight with Dale. Maybe she should go back and try to make up with him. It made her feel all wibbly-wobbly inside. She could understand that he wasn't so happy with his family. But wanting to just throw them away in favor of a bunch of people who were practically strangers to him? I mean, yeah, they were his same family. But they were different, too. They weren't his *real* family. After a little while the novelty would wear off, and Dale would realize that things had to go back to the way they had been before.

As she was walking along, she turned and looked at the house on the corner. Hadn't it been red when she walked by five minutes ago? Now it was suddenly green.

Or at least it seemed that way. She shrugged. Hey, she was probably just imagining things.

She jogged down Spruce Street and onto Main, passing by the big water tower that stood in the middle of town. It was painted to look like a sheaf of corn. She could hear Cerberus trotting along behind her. She looked back at the dog.

Then, when she turned back, the strangest thing had happened. Something felt unsettling to her. And for a moment she couldn't figure out what it was. But then it hit her: the water tower was gone. Well—not exactly *gone*. But the water tower painted to look like a giant sheaf of corn was gone. In its place was a normal-looking water tower, a large bulbous-shaped thing like the one over near the mall in Brainerd. How could that be? It had literally changed just seconds ago.

She felt a stab of fear.

The black thing at the sausage factory. Somehow the black thing was causing the universe to change. It was warping things off into some different universe. And she had the feeling that wherever it was going—well, it wasn't heading in a good direction.

"Hurry, Cerberus!" she said. And she began running faster. As she ran down Main, she noticed that the buildings seemed older and dirtier than she remembered. The building where A. Queeg's bookstore had been was boarded up and empty. Many of the shops had FOR RENT signs posted on the front. The people walking along the street seemed listless and tired.

Several large peeling posters hung on the front of one of the shops. On the poster was a picture of Bob Robbins Jr. He was looking all serious, staring into the distance. Underneath it said,

ROBBINS

FOR PRESIDENT

His Past Is Our Future.

Huh? Since when was a vacuum cleaner salesman running for president? Well, she didn't really have time to think about it.

A large black cloud drifted across the sky, dense and oppressive. Jessica hadn't noticed it before. Was it new? She could see ash filtering down over the town, tiny gray flecks.

Something was happening, definitely—something that was sucking the life out of the town. Things were veering off into a very bad place.

By the time she swung around the corner of Second Street and ran up to the library, the ash was coming down over the town like a light snow. The light from the sky, which had been clear and bright just minutes ago, had gone pale and weak.

Around the side of the library she saw a truck backed up to the loading dock. Several grim-faced men were throwing books off the loading dock into the back of the truck. Not packed in boxes or anything—just chucking them in a pile in the back, like they were just trash.

As she jogged up to the library, a man wearing a stained pair of overalls was stretching a piece of yellow caution tape across the front of the building. The huge bronze front doors of the building, normally wide open, were closed. Or almost closed anyway: one was shut tight, but the other one was wedged open about a foot with a rubber door-stopper.

"What's going on?" Jessica said to the worker.

He turned, looked at her, and shrugged. "Tearing her down," he said. The man had a thick accent that she couldn't quite place. Eastern European, maybe?

"What do you mean, tearing it down?"

"Library closed. Tearing her down."

Jessica stared at him. Was he serious? No doubt he was. She headed toward the front door, started pushing her way through the gap.

"Hey! You can't go in there!" The man's voice followed her. "Hey! Hey!"

Cerberus growled loudly.

"Hey! Get that dog out of here."

She slid through the door. Cerberus followed. Inside, the air smelled stale. There was a fine haze of dust over everything. The big lobby was completely empty.

She ran over to the reference desk, her footsteps echoing in the marble-floored room. It seemed like a mausoleum now. Nobody at the desk. She ran over to the checkout desk. Nobody there either.

"Where is everybody?" she yelled. "Hello?"

No answer. Nothing but echoes.

Cerberus looked around the room, his ears pinned back, his hackles rising.

"What is it, Cerberus?" Jessica said.

But the dog just kept his eyes glued on the far door. Jessica walked quickly toward the door. Cerberus followed. But the hair was still standing up on his neck.

As they entered the next room. Jessica spotted a bunch of older kids. What were they doing here? She recognized them as the trombone section from the high school band. Eric Ricci's brother John. Susan Something-or-other. A couple of others. They started walking toward her.

"Hey," Jessica said. "What are you guys doing in here? Is anybody still working here? I'm trying to find the director."

The older kids turned and looked at her. Then they just started walking across the large empty room. "Jumpin' Jehoshaphat, look at the size of that dog," John Ricci said, smiling.

"By cracky, you're one persistent little gal," Susan Whatever-her-name-is said.

Jessica felt her stomach turn. She could see their eyes

now, the black shadows flickering and dancing. They were all smiling like they'd just won the lottery.

"But it's all jake now," one of the other boys said. "Our friend Bob has it all under control now."

"Don't let them touch me, Cerberus," she said.

Cerberus lowered his head and growled. The kids stopped moving now, eyeing the dog. They didn't look nervous, though. They were all still smiling.

"It's almost over now," Eric Ricci's brother said. "There's not a soul that can stop it."

Susan nodded. "Not even you, little Jessie."

"Stop what?" Jessica said.

"Come now," one of the other boys said. "You know exactly."

"No, I don't."

"The text is being cleansed . . ."

". . . purged . . ."

". . . purified . . ."

". . . expurgated."

They edged closer as they spoke.

"Cerberus!" Jessica felt panic rising.

The dog lunged at Susan Whatever-her-name-was. She stepped back a pace or two.

"Oh, come now, there's no need of that," Eric Ricci's brother said. "We mean you no harm."

The tallest boy in the group hadn't spoken yet. As she recalled, he was captain of the marching band. "You're an error in the text, Jessica," he said. "An erratum. And by golly it's high time the errata were purged, wouldn't you say?"

Cerberus snapped at the boy. He backed up.

"Come on, chums," he said. "Let's get back to practice." He lifted his hand. "Fooorrrrrrrrmation, HUP! Smartly now, fellahs!"

The kids in the trombone section all lined up at attention.

"And a-one and a-two . . ."

The kids started marching across the room. They started making trombone noises and pantomiming trombones in the air. It was that song again, the same thing that people had been singing all day. The one that Jessica kept thinking she recognized, but that she just couldn't remember the name of.

"Hey!" she yelled. "What's that song?"

The captain held up his hand, and the trombone section stopped marching. The boy turned and said, "Why, Jessie, surely you know. It's 'The Battle of Bluntwick March,' of course," he said. "By the incomparable John Philip Smimza."

John Philip Smimza? He meant John Philip *Sousa*, right? "What are you *talking* about?" she said.

"It's Bob Robbins's campaign theme song," he said. "We've been asked to perform before the speech. So we're practicing."

"What speech?"

"Bob Robbins *Junior*." He kept looking at her without

blinking, the shadows leaping and dancing in his eyes. "Surely you knew that Bob Robbins was coming today. He's giving the big speech. Here. In Alsberg. He's announcing his plan to end all the problems."

With that, the kids in the trombone section turned and began marching across the room.

"Let's go, Cerberus," Jessica said. "There must be somebody here who can help us. Let's go find the director."

She ran back into the other room to try the elevator. But a small sign hung on the brass grating:

∽ⓔ Temporarily Out of Order ⓔ∽

Below it gaped a large black hole.

"Stairs!" she said.

Cerberus was ahead of her, though, already charging toward the door. They ran up the stairs together, the eerie sound of the trombone section fading behind them.

At the top of the stairs Jessica ran out into a long dim corridor. A lone figure was moving slowly toward her and Cerberus. She only hoped it wouldn't be another one of those shadow-eyed people. "Hello?" she called.

"Hello," a voice replied.

"Who's that?" Jessica said.

"It's Olaf. The janitor."

She made out his thick, dull features. He was slowly pushing a broom toward her.

"Where's the director?" she called.

There was a pause. "Gone," he said.

"Gone where?"

"He retired. Florida or someplace."

"Is there anybody left here?"

"Just me."

"Nobody at all? No librarians?"

He shook his head.

"What about the books?"

"They're carrying them off."

"Where?"

He shrugged vaguely. "There's a fire on the edge of town. They're loading them on trucks and dumping them in the fire."

"What! They can't! There's all those . . . all those beautiful books down there! Rare books. Famous books."

Olaf shrugged. "They said they don't need no books no more. President Robbins is coming to solve all the problems. So they don't need 'em no more."

President Robbins? Now he was the president? "But—"

"President Robbins says books cause problems." Olaf turned away. "I gotta keep sweeping. It's my job."

"There's nobody here? Nobody at all?"

Olaf didn't stop pushing the broom. "Maybe down in Special Collections. Miss Russell. She said she wouldn't leave."

"What floor?"

"Subbasement seven."

Olaf disappeared around the corner, still leaning on the broom.

Jessica was starting to despair now. Things were changing so fast now, she'd probably never make it. Whatever it was she was supposed to do once she got the book out of the quarry, it would probably be too late. Just like those freaks in the trombone section said.

She ran into the stairs again. Cerberus's footsteps echoed along with hers as she descended. She was still running, but her breath was coming in gasps. Maybe it was all the running. But it felt like more than that. A strange lethargy was creeping through her limbs—a feeling like it didn't really matter that much what happened.

Come on! she told herself. *Fight!*

She burst through the door of subbasement seven, found herself in the middle of a huge empty space. Hundreds of high metal shelves had been pushed haphazardly against the walls. There was not a single book left in the whole room.

Other than the empty shelves there was nothing in the room at all—nothing but a single wooden desk at the far end of the room. She ran toward it. As she approached the desk a very small, very elderly woman lifted her head from the desktop. It looked like she'd been napping.

"Yes?" she said.

"Mrs. Russell?"

"Miss," the woman said. "It's *Miss* Russell." She felt

around, as though she couldn't see very well. Then she found her glasses and lifted them carefully onto her nose. "Ah!" she said. "It's you. I was beginning to be afraid."

"What's going on?" Jessica said. "Olaf says they're burning all the books."

The woman was extremely old. She looked fragile as paper, a blue spidery vein sticking up in her forehead, hair white and wispy. She smiled gently. "Yes. They are."

"Why? What are they doing?"

"Books hold our memory," the woman said. "They're taking our memory first."

"*Who's* taking our memory? Bob Robbins?"

"Once we've forgotten, then they'll take the rest."

"The rest of what?"

The old woman looked absently around the room. "Sorry? What?"

"The rest of what? They'll take the rest of what?"

"I'm sorry, dear," the old woman said. "It goes in and out, my memory. One minute I'm sharp as a tack. The next?" She shrugged.

"Please! Think! They'll take the rest of what?"

The old woman cocked her head. "I thought you knew, dear. Didn't they tell you? They're taking it all."

"All of what?"

The old woman waved her hand vaguely in the air. "This."

Jessica was getting frustrated now. "The library?"

The old woman grinned. "No, no. The whole thing. The world. The universe. Whatever you want to call it."

"That doesn't make sense."

The old woman peered at Jessica. "They really must have told you."

"No!"

"Hm." Miss Russell gestured at a chair that sat in front of the desk. "Sit. I see there are quite a few things that need to be explained."

"The director told me all this destiny stuff. He told me that this book was really powerful. That I could change things. But he didn't tell me what I was supposed to do."

"The director." She raised one eyebrow. "Well, the first director of the library, Dr. Emerson Mills—he was a great man. Personally selected by Alphonse Margarine himself. The second director, Mr. Seaver—well, he carried on his legacy competently enough. Dr. Purvis was the third director. Nice enough young man. But he was really not up to the job. An empty suit, I hate to say it."

"Oh."

"This isn't just any old library, you know."

"I'd sort of figured that out, I guess," Jessica said.

"It's *the* library. It's where all our memories have been collected. Mr. Margarine was a genius, you know. He understood what was coming. He saw that we needed to remember. We needed to remember . . . or everything would be lost." Her voice dropped to a whisper. "Everything."

Jessica sat, waiting. When the old lady didn't speak anymore, Jessica said, "Well? What do I need to know? What am I supposed to do?"

Miss Russell sighed. "If only the director were here. Dr. Mills, I mean. He was a great, great man. A memory like an elephant."

"He's not here," Jessica said impatiently. "It's just you. Tell me what I need to know."

Miss Russell nodded. "All right, then," she said. "I'll try." She took a long deep breath. "Have you ever heard of dark energy?"

XXVI

Dale went downstairs and watched TV for a while. After a few minutes he started smelling smoke. He wondered vaguely what was burning. But he didn't wonder *that* much. It felt fine just sitting there watching the show on TV. He felt like he'd seen the show before, but he couldn't really remember. And he didn't really care, either.

After a while someone knocked on the front door. Dale kept staring at the TV. The show was about a boy and his crazy friends at school, all the crazy things they got into.

Nobody answered the door.

The knocking got louder. Finally Dale stood and opened the door.

A pleasant-looking man in a sober blue suit stood in the doorway. "Isn't it glorious, Dale?" the man said cheerfully.

The man seemed familiar. But Dale couldn't quite place him. Wasn't he that guy who had been running for president? Behind the man, he saw that the sky was dark with smoke. There were bits of ash flecking the shoulders of the man's coat. "Um? Do I know you?" Dale said.

"Bob Robbins Junior!" the man said, pulling open the screen door. "President of the good ol' U.S. of A!"

"Oh." Dale had a vague recollection. "Yeah, okay. I don't know where my parents are. Why don't you come back later." He turned away and walked back to the couch.

The president of the United States followed him into the room, looked at the TV for a minute. "Used to love that show," he said. "Boy, the wacky stuff that kid gets into!" He picked up the remote, switched off the television. "That said, I need to interrupt your viewing pleasure for just a brief moment."

"But . . ." Dale pointed at the TV. He felt like he was moving in slow motion.

Bob Robbins Jr. interrupted him. "Quick question, then you can get back to your excellent program."

"Okay."

"Your friend Jessica."

"She's not my friend," Dale said. He remembered having an argument with her a while back. But he couldn't remember what it was about. Something to do with the plastic that was duct-taped over the front window of the house? He wasn't sure.

"Okay, well, your *ex*-friend, Jessica. Did she tell you where the book is?"

"The book." Dale just wanted to watch his show again. The kid in the show was supposed to take this thing to this place, but this other thing had happened and so the thing had gotten switched around with the other thing, and everybody thought the thing was the other thing, and so now the people at the place were all mad and stuff. It was really hilarious.

"The book. *Her Lif.* The first edition with the erratum slip."

"Oh. Yeah." Dale had no clue what this guy was talking about.

"Did she tell you where it was?"

Dale scratched his head. His mind just felt so weird and fuzzy. "I . . . I think so."

"Concentrate, ol' buddy, ol' pal! Where is it?"

Dale looked out the plastic-covered window. The smoke was getting heavier, thicker, blacker. He felt some kind of alarm go off in his mind. But he ignored it. "She said something about scuba gear."

"Scuba gear?" Bob Robbins Jr. looked puzzled.

Dale nodded. "She wanted to go get some scuba gear. But I wanted to watch TV."

"Hey, who doesn't?" Bob Robbins Jr. smiled. "But where was she going to use it?"

Dale shrugged. He wasn't really interested.

"Stop looking over my shoulder at the TV, you little cretin!" Bob Robbins Jr. said sharply. And suddenly he didn't seem like such a nice guy anymore. "Concentrate! Where's the book?"

Dale suddenly felt a little scared. His pulse started beating harder. And as it did, his mind cleared a little. The quarry. She'd told him the book was in the rock quarry.

"Where is it?" Bob Robbins Jr. didn't change in any outward way. And yet suddenly he seemed stronger, older, more dangerous. "Tell me!"

"The quarry," Dale said. "I think she said it was at the quarry. In the water or something."

Just then Dale's father walked into the room. "Hey!" he shouted. "What's going on here?"

Bob Robbins's face settled into its pleasant grin. "Me and Dale are just fooling around."

Dale's father looked at Bob Robbins. "I don't know what you're doing in my house, sir. But I think you need to leave. Now."

Bob Robbins Jr. pointed his finger at Dale, making a gun with his hand. He brought his thumb down and made a loud click with his tongue. "We'll talk later, hoss!" he said brightly.

Then he disappeared out the door.

"Who was that guy?" Dale's father said, closing the door.

"I don't know," Dale said.

"Strange." Dale's father stared fixedly out the window. "Boy, if I didn't know better, I'd have thought that was President Robbins."

"Thanks, Dad," Dale said. "I really didn't like that guy."

Dale's father suddenly looked back at his son. "That's what I'm here for, son," he said.

Dale felt his pulse start to settle back to normal. "Can I watch some more TV?" he said.

His father stood silently for a minute, like he was remembering something. "Actually, not now, son," he said finally. "You need to come with me."

"Where?"

His father seemed confused for a moment. "Downtown," he said. "Everybody in the town's going to be there."

"What for?"

His father didn't answer.

XXVII

"D ark energy," the ancient librarian repeated to Jessica. "Do you know what it is?"

"Not really, no," Jessica said.

"We now know that the universe is full of alternative possibilities. Each possibility leads to an entirely new universe. You make one little change and then that causes something else and that causes something else. . . . If I choose to eat Wheaties for breakfast instead of bacon and eggs, that affects somebody at the grocery store. Which affects somebody else, which affects somebody else. And so on and on and on. Eventually an airplane crashes or an empire falls or a sun winks out."

"Oh, come on," Jessica said.

"I'm just saying, sometimes little choices have big consequences. Consequences you can't anticipate. Sure, many choices have no serious effect on things at all. But others have a huge effect."

"Okay, so Dr. Purvis told me all this stuff before. The universe is like a big road. And all these other roads fork off every time you make a decision. And then you have two different universes—one for each decision."

"That's exactly right. Now most of those universes are dead ends. Or they diverge and then converge again. But plenty of them go off on their own path. In a certain way, all these universes touch one another. So it's possible—in theory—for one universe to pass into another. It takes a great deal of energy, though. Dark energy."

"Okay."

"When something passes from one universe into another, it simply seems to disappear. Converted into nothingness. When something gets converted into nothing? The stuff you use to make that happen is dark energy."

"But you can't just make something totally disappear. That's impossible."

"Within any given universe? That's right. But something can be made to disappear here and reappear somewhere else. In another universe, say. But the problem is that things get out of balance. Dark energy is hard to control. Bob Robbins has summoned that thing up. But he really has no idea how to control it. As the universes get further and further out of balance, that dark thing will get bigger and bigger. Eventually it will get so big that it will start to endanger the entire universe. All the universes, you might say."

"But that's what I keep asking. How do you stop it?"

"Once it reaches a certain size—you can't."

"So how can we stop it before it gets that big?"

Miss Russell smiled wanly. "It's probably too late. It's already gotten that big."

Jessica slammed her fist on the desk in frustration. "Then it can't be stopped. So why am I even worrying about it?"

Miss Russell's face seemed even older, her skin more wrinkled, her cheeks sunken. For a moment her eyes glazed over. But then she leaned forward slightly and whispered, "There is a way."

"I don't understand. If you can't stop it—"

"You have to make it unhappen."

Jessica was feeling frustrated. She felt like a dog chasing her tail. The whole thing just went around and around, but never made any sense.

"It has to have never happened in the first place."

"But that's impossible!" Jessica was shouting and waving her arms now.

"You have to remember. You have to remember a universe in which Bob Robbins never unleashed the dark thing." The lights flickered above them, like something was wrong with the electricity in the building.

"But *how*? You can't remember something that never happened to you."

"But it *did* happen to you, Jessica. That's the whole point. You just have to remember it."

"No, it didn't!" Jessica was feeling angry now—so angry and frustrated, she was about ready to cry.

"The book will tell you what you need to know."

"But the book's sunk in a lake!"

"Then you'd better go get it."

"But—"

The old woman stood. There wasn't a desk anymore. The entire vast room was empty. "You've got to hurry, young lady. Get the book. You'll figure it out."

The lights flickered and snapped again. This time they went out for several seconds.

"Go!" Miss Russell shouted. "Go!"

Dale and his father found themselves in a crowd that was streaming across the town. It looked like everybody in Alsberg was in the streets now. The smoke was so heavy that it blotted out the sun completely.

Where are they going? Dale wondered. There was a look of urgency on the faces of everybody in the crowd. Women were carrying babies. Kids were pushing old people in wheelchairs. No one spoke. It seemed like the entire town was on foot.

"Where are we going?" Dale said.

His father didn't say anything.

"And why isn't anybody driving?"

His father looked at him curiously. "We haven't had gas here in a month. You know that, Dale." He frowned. "Or . . . maybe it's been a year?"

"Why not?"

"The war, Dale," his father said. "The *war*. Why are you acting so stupid?"

Dale looked at his father. He seemed haggard and drawn and irritable again. Like his father back in . . . Back in . . . *what?*

Dale squinted against the smoke. It was the strangest thing. For just a moment it seemed like he'd lived some other life. Before the war. Before the gas ran out. Before the library caught fire. He looked over and saw the burning hulk where the library had been. Flames rose high into the air. One of the walls tipped over and collapsed in a shower of sparks, only to be obscured by smoke. Buildings were burning around them everywhere. The whole city was burning!

There were no lights anywhere. No streetlights, no lamps lit in the windows of houses, nothing. The smoke was getting darker and heavier, and now he was having trouble breathing.

And then suddenly he saw it looming up in front of them. The sausage factory. There were still lights in the sausage factory. Giant beams of light that projected up into the smoke. By the time Dale and his father reached the parking lot, the crowd had already trampled over the fence surrounding the factory and were streaming toward it.

A voice was blasting across the parking lot over a loudspeaker. A stage had been set up near the entrance to the factory, with massive speakers on the sides, like a rock concert. Behind them was a giant video screen.

"Right this way!" the voice said. "Right this way! Step

right over here. Take your places!" The voice seemed familiar. A man—enthusiastic and full of energy.

The man appeared on the video screen now. His face about thirty feet tall. Dale recognized him. It was Bob Robbins Jr.! The president of the United States!

Dale felt a stab of excitement. Bob Robbins was the most famous man in America! Bob Robbins Jr.—the man who had promised to save them from the war, from the fires, global warming, pollution, unhappiness. All the world's problems, Bob Robbins Jr. had the answer.

Dale and his father moved forward. The crowd had begun to collect around the stage. There was a palpable sense of excitement. Dale and his father stopped moving now. As if in sudden agreement, the entire crowd stopped moving. There was a slogan on the huge video screen.

Our Past. Our President. Our Future.

For a moment the world seemed completely still. There was no sound at all, no sound but the soft buzzing of the huge loudspeaker system.

On the stage, Bob Robbins Jr. spread his arms. His giant face beamed from the video screen, a huge warm smile spreading across it. For the first time in—how long had it been?—Dale felt safe. All the troubles were going to go away now. Bob Robbins Jr. was going to save them.

"Welcome!" Bob Robbins slowly turned, aiming his

smile across the crowd. "Welcome, my friends." He lowered his arms, and then his smile faded. He looked out into the camera with great sincerity. "It's been a long journey, my friends. But the great day of our salvation has finally arrived."

A murmur ran across the crowd.

"The sadness? The pain? The difficulties? We've all felt them, haven't we? Sons lost in combat? Daughters in the work camps? Parents lost because they couldn't get their medicine anymore?" He nodded sadly. "I understand. Like you, I have suffered greatly in these terrible times. I have walked the same dark road as all of you. But I have found solace in knowing that we must pass through the valley of the shadow of death before we reach the promised kingdom."

Another murmur, this one louder than the last. A woman next to Dale was weeping, the tears leaving bright tracks in the ashy darkness of her face.

"My friends, the hour is at hand. The time of troubles is about to pass away like"—he looked around, as though searching for the right metaphor—"like smoke in the wind."

And as he spoke those words a gust of wind hit the crowd and—for one brief moment—the smoke cleared.

And in that moment Dale saw it: rising from the center of the sausage factory was a huge dark ball of nothing, ten stories high at least. The entire audience craned their necks upward and gasped. Dale felt a clammy, sick feeling in the pit of his stomach. Then the smoke drifted back, and the dark thing was gone.

"Do not fear it!" Bob Robbins Jr. said. "Do not fear it, because it is the end of all your pain."

The crowd stood in silence for a long time. Bob Robbins Jr. didn't move. He was staring off into the distance now, as if in rapt attention to something that no one else could see.

And then, imperceptibly at first, the smoke began to clear for good.

XXVIII

When Jessica left the library, she was shocked. The entire town was choked with smoke. Here and there a building was on fire. As she burst out the front door, she noticed smoke coming out of one window of the library. Then, when she looked back a moment later, the entire building was in flames.

She ran as fast as she could, heading back toward Coach Slocum's house. As she ran people began filtering out of their houses. No one seemed to notice her. They were just walking down the street, faces intent, heading in the general direction of the sausage factory. The smoke was making her lungs burn. She coughed hard. Cerberus followed her, sneezing repeatedly. His tongue was hanging out. Apparently the smoke was bothering him, too.

As she ran up to Coach Slocum's house, the coach came out the front door. For some reason he was bald again. His ridiculous toupee—or hair weave or whatever it was—was now gone.

"Coach!" she called. "The gear! Have you got the scuba gear?"

He looked at her curiously. "The what?"

"Scuba gear. You were going to get me some scuba gear."

He ran his hand across his bald head, a puzzled expression on his face.

"Remember? You needed more verticality in the paint? We had a deal!"

For a moment he looked puzzled. Then he said, "Jess, I haven't scuba dived for eight, ten years. Not since before the war."

Jess felt sick. "But, coach . . ."

"I have to go," he said. "We all have to go."

"Where?"

"To the sausage factory. It was just on the TV. Bob Robbins Junior is finally going to—" He looked confused. He shook his head. "I have to go. I have to go."

And then he walked swiftly up the street, his too-tight pants making a *sipp-sipp-sipp* sound as he walked.

For a moment Jessica felt like crying. No scuba gear? How was she going to . . . And then something struck her. In this universe—unlike the one she'd been in twenty minutes ago—Coach Slocum *had* scuba dived.

On any normal day, she wouldn't have considered going into somebody's house uninvited. But this really wasn't a normal day, was it?

"Stay, Cerberus," she said to the dog. It lay obediently on the dry, brown lawn.

She ran into Coach Slocum's house. It was exceedingly

neat, with knotty pine–paneled walls hung with pictures of basketball players. She saw a closet door, yanked it open. Inside were neatly stacked plastic bins, each one carefully labeled. TROPHIES, SWEATERS, WRAPPING PAPER, ELECTRICAL CORDS, TINFOIL.

Tinfoil? The guy kept *tinfoil* in a closet?

But no scuba equipment.

She searched the bedroom closets. Nothing.

Nothing in the bathroom, nothing in the den. As she came out of the third bedroom, the smell of smoke suddenly intensified. She ran out into the living room. The house was on fire! The drapes were ablaze, and the couch was erupting like a volcano of flame.

She tried to get to the front door, but the heat was so ferocious she felt like she was going to be burned alive. Panic rose inside her.

What was she going to do? She could barely breathe from the smoke. What was it they always said? Get down on the ground and crawl. The smoke rises, so the good air is always on the ground.

She lay down on the floor and began creeping through the kitchen. It worked. The air was much better there. More oxygen, less smoke. She scanned the room. There must be another way out of the house.

Something in the back of the house went WHOOMPH, like a small explosion. *Hurry! Hurry!* Now even the air down on the floor was getting bad. And the heat was intensifying.

Wait.

There! There was a door.

She stood, yanked it open. Cool air spilled over her. On the other side of the door, she saw the garage. Inside was Coach Slocum's pride and joy, his car—a Corvette, covered with a clear plastic car cover. Against the far wall hung a neat row of gardening implements. On the floor were more stacks of plastic bins. Next to the door hung a row of keys, each one neatly labeled. On the other side of the keys was a switch for the garage door. She pounded it with her fist. But nothing happened.

There was no power!

How was she going to get out?

There was a window on the far side of the room. A small window, high up on the wall. She ran over to it, tried to climb up. But it was too high. She grabbed a stack of bins, shoved them against the wall.

Smoke was starting to curl under the door from the house. *Hurry, Jess!* she thought. *Hurry!* She climbed onto the bins. They immediately collapsed.

Stupid, cheap bins! Jessica felt tears running down her face. Not only had she failed at finding the scuba gear, but she was going to be burned alive because. . . .

Suddenly she stopped and stared. One of the bins that had just spilled open was labeled SCUBA EQUIPMENT.

She yanked it open. Inside was a yellow air tank, a belt with a bunch of little weights hanging off of it, and a diving mask.

Yes!

Her momentary burst of excitement dimmed. It wouldn't do any good to have the scuba junk if she burned to death in here. She looked around the room for something she could climb on. But there was nothing. Nothing but the car. And it was too far away from the window.

Suddenly something struck her. *The car!* Maybe the car would be the answer to her problems. All she had to do was start it up and smash through the garage door with it. Her grandfather used to take her out in the fields of his farm over near Long Prairie and let her drive the tractor. If she could drive a tractor, she could surely back a Corvette through a garage door.

She ran over to the row of hooks on the wall, checked the labels on the keys. SHED. BACK DOOR. FRONT DOOR. There it was!—'VETTE.

She grabbed the key, pulled the tarp off the car, jumped in, and cranked the engine. It made a dull coughing noise. But the car wouldn't start.

Then she remembered something. There hadn't been a single car on the roads after she left the library. There was some kind of gasoline shortage now, wasn't there?

She jumped out of the car, looked around the garage. Coach Slocum was a very neat guy, very well prepared. What if . . .

There it was. A red gas can. She grabbed it, picked it up, shook it. There must have been about a cupful of gas inside. That was enough, though, wasn't it? She didn't have to go very far.

She unscrewed the gas cap on the car, poured the gas into the tank, threw the red can on the floor, and jumped in. Her heart was racing as she tried the key.

Nothing. Just the same terrible coughing noise.

She pumped the gas pedal. "Come on!" she shouted. "Come on!"

This time the big motor roared to life.

"Yes!" she shouted, punching the air with her fist.

She found the shifter knob, wobbled it around until it was next to the big red R, then ducked her head down and stomped on the gas. The powerful car leaped backward, smashing through the door like it was made of paper.

Cerberus was still lying in the yard.

She pulled open the door of the car. Then she ran back inside the garage, grabbed the bin full of scuba gear, hurled it into the car, and jumped into the driver's seat.

It had just occurred to her that the car might have another use for her. She had to find a way to get to the quarry and back.

She looked over at Cerberus. The big dog looked back at her, then cocked its head. It was almost as though it was asking her a question: *Are you really going to steal this car?* Or maybe he was wondering, *Could she actually drive this thing?*

"Well, Cerberus," she said, patting the dog on the head, "we're about to find out, huh?"

She stomped on the gas again. The car jumped backward, slamming into a garbage can. She'd forgotten to shift it into the gear that would make it go forward.

"Oops," she said. Then she started to laugh.

Stealing a car! She couldn't believe it. Goody-goody Jessica Sternhagen, *stealing* a car?

Definitely hard to believe. But honestly? It was pretty fun. She looked at the shifter. There were a bunch of numbers next to the lever—1, 2, and 3. Also an N and a D. Which was the right one? She wrestled it to the one that said 1, carefully pressed the accelerator. The car began to move. Yes! She grinned fiercely. Now all she had to do was keep it on the road. And how hard could that be?

She drove through the deserted, smoke-clogged streets. The car made a very high-pitched whine like the engine was racing—but it didn't seem to want to go very fast. Which was okay.

Suddenly she felt sad. She just wished Dale were there with her. Things were always so much better when he was around.

XXIX

"T hank you!" Bob Robbins Jr. called to the crowd. "Thank you for your trust and your support and, yes, your love. I'm here with you in Alsberg, Minnesota. But our little gathering today is being beamed worldwide via satellite."

As the smoke began to lift, Dale looked around. The crowd was much larger than he had imagined. Much larger than it seemed like it had been just a few minutes ago, stretching as far as he could see in all directions. There were a lot of people he didn't recognize – people with backpacks on their backs, like they had hiked great distances to get here. There were news crews here and there, using precious battery power to beam Bob Robbins's message of hope out to the wider world. Dale felt privileged to be present at this extraordinary moment.

A few ragged wisps of smoke wafted by.

And then the sky was entirely clear.

Other than the sausage factory—and the great dark shape looming up over it—there was nothing around them at all. The town seemed to have been entirely consumed.

There were no buildings standing. Other than one broken, smoldering wall of the library, the town had entirely ceased to exist. Around the huge crowd, the gently rolling prairie extended in all directions, unbroken to the horizons.

It must have looked like this two hundred years ago, Dale thought. Back before . . . But then he couldn't quite put his finger on what had happened here. Back before . . . what?

Above everything, the sky was blue and clear and empty. Not a cloud, not a bird, not a jet contrail. Just an empty, stainless expanse of blue. He turned back and looked at Bob Robbins.

"Yes, my children," Bob Robbins Jr. said. Now the giant TV screen was offering simultaneous translation, words crawling across the bottom—German, French, Russian, Chinese. "You have come long, long distances to join me here. You have faced unimaginable terrors and hardships. Hunger, thirst, tired muscles, sore feet, sickness, snowstorms, and hurricanes. Perhaps even the loss of loved ones. But your time of sadness is over. Now is your time of wholeness and completion."

Dale felt a warmth spreading through him as he listened to Bob Robbins Jr. He smiled. Wasn't this nice? No more problems. He took a deep breath. The air smelled clean and fresh and fragrant.

"My friends, all you have to do is forget. Learning things is so hard. Times tables. Verses of poetry. Dates of treaties. Names of presidents and kings. Come on! Does anyone really care whether three times three is nine? Or ten?

Or four?" He smiled broadly. "I don't. Does anyone care who won the Battle of Bluntwick? Not me! Faces. Places. Names. Addresses. It's all the same really. Just let go. Forget them all."

A soft, inarticulate noise rose from the crowd. Dale realized that people were crying now. They were smiling and crying at the same time.

"Yes!" Bob Robbins called out. "Yes! You feel it, don't you! All the pain is passing away from you. You're forgetting how to do your job. You're forgetting about how you got sent to the principal in second grade because you refused to learn your times tables. You're forgetting about the science fair. You're forgetting who the first president of the United States was. You don't need it! You don't need to remember *anything*! You don't need to *know* anything!"

As Dale was listening, he looked up for the first time in several minutes and saw that the sausage factory was completely gone. Nothing was left but the great black sphere. And now the sphere was changing. Not just growing, but throbbing imperceptibly, beating like a giant dark heart. Dale wasn't sure why, but something about it filled him with terror.

What was it he was supposed to forget? Was he supposed to forget to be afraid? Was that what Bob Robbins Jr. was really getting at?

"In a few minutes, the treasure will come to us," Bob Robbins Jr. said. "The transformation will happen. And then we'll forget forever."

A gust of wind blew across the crowd, just a hint of winter chill in it. Which was strange, since it was late May. Bob Robbins's necktie fluttered and snapped in the wind.

The only sounds were the wind, and the hum of the sound system. Dale noted that the humming of the sound system had begun to take on a rhythm. A rhythm that matched the pulsating of the great black sphere that rose now, hundreds of feet into the sky.

And then someone in the front of the crowd yelled something. "What is it?" the voice said, barely audible even from where Dale was standing.

Bob Robbins turned and looked up at the dark thing. On the TV screen he smiled fondly. "It's nothing," he said. "It's nothing at all." He spread his hands. "You see, friends, all our lives we've been filling our minds with details. We go to school, and they cram our heads with facts and figures and theorems and formulas. We go home and our mothers and fathers stuff us with chores and responsibilities and family pictures and boring stories about when they were little girls and boys. Then we get jobs, and the boss tells us we need to remember this appointment and accomplish that goal in such and such a way and . . ." He sighed loudly. "It's foolish."

"Why?" It was the same voice.

Bob Robbins looked a little irritated. "Why?" he said sarcastically. "Why!" He looked around the crowd. "You believe this guy? Could there possibly, on the entire planet, be a dumber question than that?"

The crowd laughed. Dale laughed, too. But for reasons he couldn't quite fathom, he felt uncomfortable.

"Why?" the tiny voice called again. "Why is it foolish to remember?"

Bob Robbins's face darkened. "Okay, now I'm starting to get annoyed. All these nice people came here to be transformed. And you're asking *why*? What kind of monster are you?"

The crowd rumbled.

Someone next to Dale muttered, "Shut him up."

"Yeah," somebody else said, louder this time. "Shut him up!"

"Shut him up!" Another voice, shouting, choked with anger. "Shut him up!"

Bob Robbins Jr. held up his hands, and the crowd quieted. "I am sorry to say it, my friends. But there are traitors among us."

Somewhere in front of him a man was starting to push through the crowd. He seemed to be moving in Dale's general direction. A traitor! Dale felt alarmed. What if the traitor got near him? What would he do?

A head was moving through the crowd.

"Let him go," Bob Robbins said scornfully. "The poor guy's delusional. He thinks one man can change things. Fine. Go ahead, buddy! We don't need you anyway."

People were pushing and shoving the man, spitting at him, saying nasty things. But he kept moving. Closer and closer. Dale could see his face now. The man looked very frightened. His face was gaunt, and his clothes were torn. He looked very afraid.

As he approached Dale, Dale shrank back. Someone pushed the man. He stumbled, brushing up against Dale as he struggled to regain his balance.

And as he righted himself, the man pressed something into Dale's hand. Dale couldn't bring himself to look at what the man had given him.

The man kept going, but the crowd was getting angrier, louder.

"Traitor! Traitor!" The call started with one or two people, then grew louder and louder. "Traitor! Traitor! TRAITOR!"

Soon the entire crowd was swaying back and forth, chanting the words.

And then, suddenly, like a bubble popping on the surface of a glass of milk, the man's head disappeared. There was a brief disturbance—some rapid motions in the vicinity of where the man had disappeared—and then the crowd grew still and the chanting faded. The man was gone. The crowd turned and looked expectantly back at Bob Robbins Jr.

He stood there silently in the breeze, expressionless.

"Did something just happen?" Bob Robbins said finally, looking around a little blankly.

The crowd was silent.

There was a brief pause. Dale felt vaguely uncomfortable. For some reason he was feeling much clearer in his mind now. He remembered *exactly* what had just happened. The man fighting through the crowd. The angry faces. Dale looked at Bob Robbins Jr. and was quite sure that Bob Robbins knew and remembered it just as exactly as he did. It struck him with sudden and powerful force that Bob Robbins Jr. was a phony. He was a big fat liar.

Bob Robbins shrugged, a little smirk crossing his blandly handsome face. "Because, frankly, my friends, I don't remember anything at all."

The crowd erupted in applause and laughter.

Why are they laughing and clapping so hard? Dale wondered. *Is it possible that everyone remembered?* Maybe that's what it was. Maybe it was because they didn't really *want* to remember that something terrible had just happened to that man. Dale's fingers clutched at the object the man had given him. He didn't want to look at it, though. He knew it would remind him of what had just happened.

Behind the stage, the great sphere wobbled for a moment, then expanded visibly.

Bob Robbins Jr. turned and looked over his shoulder. For a moment he seemed kind of nervous. But then he turned back and smiled. "It's very close, my friends. All we have to do is wait. And as long as there are no traitors, we'll be fine."

"Hey, Bob!" a woman's voice called. "How can we recognize a traitor?"

"Great question," Bob Robbins Jr. said. "It's easy. A traitor will have one of these." He held up his hand. In his hand was a book. On the screen Dale could see the cover, magnified about a hundred times. It read: *The Reader's Digest Book of Jokes.*

The crowd gasped.

"Other than this one, so far as I know, there's only a couple or three books left. If you see someone with a book, you need to get that book from them, folks. You need to get it from the traitor. And you need to give it to me."

Bob Robbins scanned the crowd slowly. Dale got the impression he was searching for something. For more traitors, maybe. Dale didn't want to be a traitor. He hoped nobody had seen the traitor when he gave Dale . . . well, whatever it was that he'd given him.

Bob Robbins's eyes suddenly stopped. To his horror, Dale realized that their gazes had met. The great man was staring straight at him. And something in his eyes made Dale feel very afraid. A cold emptiness.

Unable to meet Bob Robbins's gaze, Dale looked abruptly at the ground. And as he did so, he saw the thing that the traitor had pressed into his hands as he fell.

It was a book.

XXX

As Jessica drove along the deserted highway, the smoke slowly began to clear and the sky went blue again. She had the pedal pressed to the floor, but the car wouldn't go more than about twenty-five miles an hour. She was pretty sure a sports car should go a lot faster than that. But she didn't know what to do about it. The engine made a loud whining noise. Something was definitely not right. But she wasn't sure what it was.

She'd gotten about halfway out toward the quarry when it occurred to her that maybe she had put the gearshift lever in the wrong place. She wasn't sure if you could shift while you were driving, so she pulled off to the side and looked at the letters and numbers next to the shifter. D, that probably stood for *drive*, right? She gingerly moved the shifter to the letter D, then pressed the accelerator to the floor. The tires let out a terrible shriek, then the car threw her back in the seat, and spun around. Within seconds, she found herself in a ditch. A cloud of black, stinky smoke surrounded her.

"Oh my God," she said. "Oh my God, Cerberus, I think I broke it!"

She pressed the accelerator gently, just in case. And to her relief the car eased slowly out of the ditch. Her heartbeat slowed a little. Soon the car was up to forty-five. That seemed plenty fast.

Within minutes, she had reached the quarry.

She threw the oxygen tank and the weight belt over her shoulder. It was really heavy.

"Let's go, boy," she said.

The hike to the quarry didn't take long. Soon she was standing at the edge of the cliff, looking down at the placid blue surface of the water. It made her woozy looking down. She didn't like heights, not even a little bit.

"Now what?" she said to Cerberus. There had to be a way to get down to the water. But she couldn't figure out what it was. The quarry was surrounded by sheer walls. And not only that. She really wasn't sure how to operate the scuba gear.

There was a tank with a knob on the top. A hose ran from that to the mask. But what was the point of the belt with the weights on it? That must be to keep you from floating to the surface.

She turned the knob. It let out a sharp hiss. There was a little gauge on the side of the knob. The face was divided into a green, a yellow, and a red area. She assumed that red meant empty. The needle was halfway down into the red. Not good. How much time would that give her before the air ran out. Five minutes? Ten? Fifteen? She had no idea.

She strapped on the weight belt. Boy, was it heavy! Then she put the tank on her back, tightening the straps so it fitted her snugly. Finally she slipped on the mask.

"Well, Cerberus," she said. "Here goes nothing."

She stuck the mouthpiece in, looked over the edge again. It was so far! She would die for sure. Her stomach twisted. But she had to go. She took a deep breath. Then another. Then another.

And then she jumped off the side of the cliff.

Her arms windmilled as she struggled to keep herself upright. But the tank threw off her balance. She fell for what seemed like forever.

Uh-oh, she thought as the blue water rushed upward toward her. *This was a really bad idea.*

Falling and falling and falling.

Dale felt panic rising in his chest. A traitor! Was he a traitor? A traitor to what? He certainly didn't feel like a traitor! But if he wasn't a traitor, then why did he have a book in his hand.

He quickly slipped the book under his shirt, his heart hammering in his chest. He looked up, halfway expecting to see the entire crowd turning toward him.

But they didn't. He might as well not have existed.

Suddenly all kinds of things were crowding into his head. Memories of sleeping in the broom closet under the stairs. Memories of a world where there wasn't a war or a gas shortage, where books didn't get burned, and people remembered stuff.

On the stage, Bob Robbins Jr. turned and looked at the huge dark thing again. It was expanding and contracting now. It reminded Dale of a boxer before a match, bobbing around, warming up for what was to come.

Unless Dale was totally off base, Bob Robbins Jr. looked a little nervous. The man onstage wiped his forehead.

"Where's that traitor, people?" Bob Robbins said. "We need that book! We need that book and we need it soon."

The crowd didn't speak. They just stared at him.

"Look around you, people! It's probably a girl. She's a tall girl, but she's just a girl. Very blond hair."

Jessica! They were talking about Jessica!

People in the crowd looked listlessly around them. But nobody seemed to see anything suspicious.

Bob Robbins Jr. looked over his shoulder nervously again. The big black thing was shifting and moving. It wasn't really a sphere anymore. More like a huge amoeba. "Come on! *Look*, people! Stop staring at me like I'm speaking some foreign language. Start looking for the freakin' traitor! Jeez Louise, you morons!"

Dale knew that if Bob Robbins Jr. was scared of the black thing, then he ought to be scared, too.

"Dad," Dale whispered. "We need to go."

But his father just kept staring up at the black shape, a glazed expression on his face. It reminded Dale of the shadows that had flickered in the eyes of the people in the Map Room that morning. Only there was no flickering here. Just darkness.

Dale started pushing his way through the crowd. Everyone's eyes were like his father's, dark and empty.

"Come on, people!" Bob Robbins Jr. shouted. "Pay attention to me. For cripe's sake! Find the girl. Bring me the book!"

But nobody in the crowd really seemed to be paying attention to Bob Robbins anymore.

"Hey! Listen!" Bob Robbins looked desperate now. "I'm the one in charge here! Listen to me, you idiots! I *need* that book!"

Dale started moving faster and faster. The people parted in front of him like corn in front of a harvester. They were all staring at the black thing. They didn't care about books or traitors or Bob Robbins Jr. anymore.

Dale was running now, slamming into people, heading for the edge of what used to be the town. He had to find Jessica! He had to help her! God, how could he have been so stupid? She had been right all along. This was a dead end. A dead end leading toward that horrible black thing that had now blotted out half the horizon.

A noise began to rise out of the crowd, a soft rumbling. For a moment Dale couldn't figure out what the sound was. But then he realized.

The crowd had begun to move. It was the sound of tramping feet. Where were they going?

Dale saw it then: they were beginning to walk toward the darkness.

"No!" shouted Bob Robbins Jr. "Not yet! I'm commanding you! Don't go yet!"

The speakers were crackling now, like the wires were being disconnected. People were swarming slowly up onto the stage, up and around Bob Robbins Jr., climbing over the big speakers.

"No! Not yet! I'm"—*skreeeeeeee*—"not to"—*sckreeeeeee-eeeeeeee*—"if you—"

Something had gone wrong with the speakers. They were squealing and crackling and cutting out, so you could only hear some of the words. Dale was running as fast as he could now, pushing people out of the way as the crowd surged forward.

"Don't! I'm telling you"—*skreeeeeee*—"it will destroy you. You fools, it will—"*skreeeeeeeeeeeeeee* —

And then the speakers went dead for good.

There was only the sound of shuffling feet. Dale looked over his shoulder. Bob Robbins Jr. stood on the stage, waving his arms and shouting. But he was so far away now that his voice was drowned out by the crowd.

Behind him people were climbing over everything, covering the stage like ants. For a moment Bob Robbins Jr.'s panicked face was caught on the video screen behind them. Then the screen began slowly, slowly, slowly to fall. This was getting really bad. Dale had to do something.

He remembered everything now.

The quarry! He had to get to the rock quarry! He had to help her find the book, the one about her life.

But . . . *how?* How would he get there? There was no gas here, no cars that worked.

Dale finally stopped running. With all the buildings in the town gone, he couldn't even tell if he was going in the right direction.

The crowd was still moving, people shuffling patiently forward toward the dark thing. It kind of reminded him of a zombie movie. Except these people didn't look all freaky and mad and pizza-faced. They were smiling blankly and moving patiently forward, as peaceful as lambs, their clouded eyes fixed on the growing darkness.

XXXI

Bob Robbins Jr. had been planning for this moment for a long time. A *very* long time. Within a year or two after Victor had plucked him off the farm in Moldavia and taken him away to be a magician's assistant, Bob Robbins had been planning for this. How long had it been? A little over three hundred years.

But now that it had arrived—well, it just wasn't working out the way he'd planned.

Which was making him a little frantic. Because Bob Robbins Jr. was in a unique position to know precisely how bad things could go wrong.

The front ranks of the crowd were reaching the dark thing. It was so big now that it rose like a wall out of the ground. The first few people to reach it held out their hands, as though to touch it. But then the crowd pressed forward, and the front ranks of the crowd were simply pressed into the darkness.

Where they vanished as completely as if they had never existed.

Which—if Bob Robbins understood the dark thing properly—was exactly what was happening. Back when he was a young man, Bob Robbins had believed the dark force was magic. But it wasn't, of course. It was just science, physics, whatever you wanted to call it.

The crowd was moving inexorably forward.

These *idiots*! He had brought them here to make them into his servants, his subjects, his followers. And now they were abandoning him, wandering off into oblivion. Just when he needed them.

What was he going to do? He had to stop this before . . . well, before it couldn't be stopped at all.

What was he going to do? His mind was a whirl of emotions. Rage, fear, hopelessness. Bob Robbins Jr. was a guy who was proud of always being equal to the moment. But just now—he had no ideas, no strategies, no nothing. He wanted to lie down and cry like a baby.

His reverie was interrupted by a voice at his shoulder: "My goodness, Mr. Robbins. You really didn't play this one so marvelously, did you?"

Bob Robbins Jr. whirled. A thin dapper man stood next to him, looking mildly up at the dark thing. He wore a tuxedo and carried a gold-headed cane.

Bob Robbins stared at him.

"That's a big 'un, isn't it?" the thin man said. "Biggest I've ever seen. By a large margin. A doozy, I'd say would be the word. *Doozy?* Hm? How does that word sit with you?"

Bob Robbins Jr. glared at the thin man. "Who are you?"

"Allow me to introduce myself." The man bowed slightly, then extended a card printed on fine cream-colored stock. His manner reminded Bob Robbins of somebody from maybe a hundred and fifty, two hundred years ago.

Bob Robbins Jr. read the card.

Elwig P. Craven III, PH.D., FRSE, *etc.*
Lingual Engineer

Bob Robbins Jr. tore the card in half and threw it on the ground.

"No, I've never seen one quite like it," the oddly dressed man said, looking up at the dark thing. "I've heard they do this, though. Before they reach the final stage."

Bob Robbins Jr. stared up at the dark thing. Tendrils had begun to reach out now, like the hands of a blind man. And wherever the tendrils went, things simply disappeared. Blades of grass, people, a truck with the logo of a twenty-four-hour news channel on the sides. Gone.

This was bad. This was *so* bad. Bob Robbins gasped, "Oh, crap."

The thin man smiled tightly. "Seven hundred and thirty-one thousand, two hundred and nine words in the English language and that's the *best* you could do? *Crap?* I don't mean to be disparaging, but after all I've heard about you? Well . . . you disappoint me, Mr. Robbins. Just a little."

Bob Robbins Jr. didn't know who this annoying guy was. But he didn't feel like standing around and finding out. In fact, Bob Robbins didn't have any idea what to do. He felt a stab of despair. What was he going to do? What was he going to *do*? He put his head in his hands. How had everything gone so wrong? All his *plans*? All his *dreams*?

The thin man pulled out a gold pocket watch, glanced at it, then looked back up at the huge wall of darkness. "Hm," he said. "We really don't have much time, you know, Mr. Robbins. An hour, perhaps? Maybe less?"

A long tendril reached out of the darkness, heading straight toward them. Bob Robbins ducked. An entire family next to him vanished. For a moment Bob Robbins was sure he was a goner.

But the tendril retreated into the dark thing again. Bob Robbins stared fearfully up at it now. He could feel it reaching out to him. Yes. Yes, maybe it would be better, just to join the others. Forget his plan. Forget what was going to happen. Forget everything.

"You know you're making a big mistake, don't you?" the man in the tuxedo said.

Bob Robbins Jr. looked at the man in irritation. "Are you still here?"

"Your mistake was, you thought you could do it without the girl. Pride cometh, my boy. Pride cometh."

"Can you just shut *up*?" Bob Robbins Jr. heard his voice coming out as a shrill scream. He hated losing control like that. But it hardly mattered now.

The thin man nudged him in the ribs with the handle of his cane.

"You'd better get the girl," Elwig P. Craven III said. "Wouldn't you say, Bob?"

XXXII

The water came up and hit Jessica like a wall of frigid bricks, snapping her body backward and smashing her head into the steel air tank.

The next thing she knew, she was drowning.

At least . . . it seemed that way. She was deep underwater. The mask was gone, ripped from her face. And so was the mouthpiece. She tried to swim up toward the light. But she couldn't. Jessica was a good swimmer. But it didn't matter. She realized that the weight belt and the air tank were making her sink. She thrashed around in panic. The dim light above her began to fade as she sank inexorably through the cold water toward the bottom.

Air! She had to have air.

Think, Jessica! Think! She tried to calm herself. *Okay, okay, okay. I still have the tank, right? And the air hose must still be attached to the tank.*

She put one hand over her shoulder, felt around until her hand hit the smooth surface of the air hose. She was seriously running out of air now, fighting the urge to gasp for breath. As her fingers followed the hose, she started seeing spots swimming in front of her eyes.

Hurry! Hurry!

She continued to sink. The air in her ears was expanding, making it feel like someone was driving nails into her head. The pain was horrible.

And then her fingers closed around the mouthpiece. She jammed it into her mouth, sucked in furiously. Air filled her lungs.

She pinched her nose shut and blew air into her ears. The pressure equalized, and the pain in her ears ceased. The water continued to drift by, though, as she sank and sank and sank. Around her everything her grew darker and darker. Colder, too.

For a moment she had the terrible notion that she might just keep sinking forever. With all the weird things that had happened to her today . . . would that be any weirder?

But then with a gentle bump, her feet hit bottom.

She looked around. Now what? It was utterly, utterly, utterly dark. Above her she could see a tiny, pale, wobbling yellow blob about the size of a dime, surrounded by blackness. The sun. Otherwise, nothing.

The cold was penetrating, making her limbs feel stiff and awkward. Desperation flooded through her. How would she ever find the book in this icy darkness?

She wondered if there was a flashlight in the car. That would mean she'd have to float back up, climb out of the quarry (not sure how she was going to do that!), go back to the car, put on all the gear again. . . . It would take a ton of time. Plus, she didn't have any air spare. If she wasted a bunch of it . . . Well, what was the alternative? Right now she was totally blind down here.

She'd have to take off the weight belt to do that, though. She felt around her middle. Searching with her frozen fingers for the clasp. But then her hand hit something. Something cylindrical attached to the belt. Could it be . . .

Yes! It was a flashlight. Inside a zippered pouch. She hadn't even noticed it before. She fumbled with the zipper.

Eventually she was able to free the light. As she searched the flashlight for a switch, it occurred to her that even with a light, this was probably a hopeless project. The pond must have covered a good ten acres. A team of professional divers working a carefully laid-out grid search probably could do it if they had a few days. But one girl? Who didn't know squat about scuba diving? And her mask had fallen off? And her air was going to run out in about two seconds?

Well, the odds were not good.

But then something struck her. She was Jessica Sternhagen, right? Girl of destiny, or whatever? She was *meant* to find the book!

She found the switch. A thin blurry beam of light uncoiled itself from her hand and thrust out into the darkness. Now she could see. And what she saw was: *brown blurriness.* She couldn't make out anything at all.

She needed the mask. Without the mask, everything was just a blur.

Well, the mask must be somewhere around here, she thought. When it fell off her head, it must have sunk, too. So it was just a matter of finding it.

She shone the beam around in a slow circle.

Hey! There was something! A bright yellow blur in the general expanse of brown. She moved slowly toward it, reached down, picked it up. Yes! The mask!

She put it over her head. It was full of water. She blew air through her nose, and the water cleared.

And—just like that—she could see. Clear as a bell. All she could see at that moment, though, was the thin beam of the light, disappearing into the darkness.

She lowered the beam of her light and shone it around her.

Her eyes widened.

Oh no, she thought, her heart sinking. *No. Not this.*

Books. As far as she could see, in every direction.

The entire bottom of the pond was covered with books. Paperback books. Hardback books. Small books. Big books. Thick books. Thin—

This was crazy! Who would have gone to the trouble to fill this entire place with books? It didn't make any sense.

Well, what could she do? She just had to start looking.

She began to half-swim, half-walk across the bottom. And as she moved, she shone the light down and scanned the books below her.

Encyclopedia Brown and the Case of the Disgusting Sneakers.

Great Sea Explorers of Portugal. Learn to Become a Model (or Just Look Like One). Welding Basics. Fulton County Blues by Ruth Birmingham. *Tort Law for Dummies. The Complete Works of Walter Savage Landor (Vol. IX).* One dumb, useless book after another.

And none of them was *Her Lif.*

Jessica felt herself growing colder and colder. She was starting to shiver now, and her head ached.

And not only that, but as she moved, she was also stirring up mud and dirt. Visibility in the water was dropping. She could only see about eight or ten feet now with all the gunk swirling around her.

She focused the beam back on the books. *Learn to Play the Ukelele for Fun and Profit. Cooking with the Barefoot Contessa. Godless* by Pete Hautman. *Steel Forming and Heat Treating. A Diplomatic History of Haiti.* The books stretched on and on.

The water was getting cloudier and cloudier. Jessica could hardly feel the flashlight anymore, and her entire body was shaking. Her breath was coming harder and harder, too.

At first she thought her breathing problems were caused by the cold.

But then she looked down at the little air gauge. The needle was all the way down into the bottom of the red now. A wave of hopelessness ran through her.

How much time did she have? A couple minutes maybe. Then she'd have to take off the weight belt, float up, and—

Whoa! What was *that*?

As the muddy water swirled around her, she thought she had seen something lying on the bottom. It looked like . . .

But no. It couldn't be. There couldn't be a *baby* lying on the bottom of the pond. But that's what it looked like. It looked like there had been a tiny—

No. No, it had to have been her imagination. She sucked in a lungful of stale air. *No one would do something that horrible! Nobody would throw a baby into a pond.*

She pointed her flashlight toward the thing that she had seen. But all she could see was silt and gunk floating lazily in the darkness.

She took a step forward. Her legs were starting to cramp from the cold, and moving around was getting harder all the time.

The air was getting harder and harder to pull in now. Jessica had to fight to get anything into her lungs. But she kept moving forward anyway.

Wait! There! A small huddled shape emerged briefly into the cone of light. Then disappeared. She staggered forward, feet slipping on the books under her.

And then she saw it again. No. It wasn't a baby. But it was human.

Lying there on the books was the smallest man she had ever seen. He couldn't have been more than two and a half feet tall. His eyes were closed. He wore a dark suit, and his hands were folded across his chest.

He could have been sleeping.

Only . . . nobody came down here to sleep. If you stayed here very long, you died.

Jessica felt the cold clamping into her bones now. She didn't want to be down here anymore. This was just too creepy, too horrible.

She sucked for air. But finally she had to admit it. There was just nothing left in the tank.

And then she saw it. A book lay splayed across the tiny dead man's chest. It looked almost as though he had been reading it and then lain down to take a nap.

It was a slightly charred leather-bound book, the edges of the pages gleaming a dull gold in the light.

Her Lif! Jessica almost screamed. It was her book! She pressed forward, leaned over the tiny man, stretched out her hand.

Slowly, painfully she closed her fingers around the book. But her muscles were so stiff and weak now that she could barely hold on to it.

As she did so, the tiny dead man's eyes suddenly blinked open. He stared up at her, a strange fixed gaze.

Jessica *did* scream then. As her scream died out, she tried to breathe in. But there was no air left. It was time to go.

Without even thinking, she shrugged off the tank, then clawed at the weight belt. Her useless fingers somehow got the clasp undone, and the belt slipped off her hips.

With that, she sudden regained buoyancy. She began to rise. Slowly at first. Then faster and faster.

The black water streamed past her. Above her the tiny pale disk of the sun grew brighter and brighter. But still, her lungs were crying out for air.

Brighter and brighter and brighter. Her ears began to hurt again as the air inside them expanded. And she needed to breathe so badly!

Hang on, Jess! she thought. *Hang on!*

And then she broke the surface, sucking desperately for air. But, as the first desperate gasp of air filled her lungs, a terrible realization struck her.

The book! She could feel that her hands were empty.

Oh no! I lost the book!

XXXIII

Dale looked through the thinning crowd, trying to figure out what he could do to find Jessica. Then he saw the answer.

Moving slowly through the people was a long black limousine, a Rolls-Royce. It was that guy, Elwig Craven, the one who had wanted to buy the book from Jessica.

Dale waved his arms. "Hey! Hey! Over here." He began running again. "Hey!"

The car slowed and then turned toward him. When it drew up next to him, the back window rolled slowly down, and the thin dapper man in the peculiar old clothes looked out at Dale. "Well, well," Elwig P. Craven III said, "if it isn't Dale McDuffie."

"We have to find Jessica," Dale said.

Elwig P. Craven smiled. "Indeed we do. Hop in, young man."

Dale shivered. It was growing noticeably colder now. Something to do with that horrible dark thing, he assumed.

He climbed into the car. As the door slammed shut,

he saw that there was another person in the car. *Oh no,* he thought. It was that Bob Robbins guy.

As though reading his thoughts, Elwig Craven said, "Don't worry about him. He's nobody."

"Yeah, but—"

"Mr. Robbins had his moment," Elwig Craven said. "As they say in the vernacular, 'He blew it.'"

"So what's going on here?" Dale said. "What is that dark thing?"

"It's a sort of tunnel, you might say," Elwig Craven said. "It's a passage through which we can communicate with other dimensions, ones that aren't precisely part of our universe."

Dale stared up at the dark thing. Long tendrils were now searching outward, absorbing people and things, sucking them up like dark tornadoes.

"What's it doing?"

"Let's get to that in a moment," Elwig Craven said. "Does Jessica have the book?"

"She's trying to get it."

"Where?"

"This old rock quarry. It's out—"

"I know exactly where it is," Elwig Craven said. Craven tapped on the divider that separated them from the driver of the vehicle. "Floyd. The quarry. Step on it!" He smiled broadly, turned to Dale again. "I love saying that."

"Okay, now can you tell me what's going on."

"It's a little hard to explain," Elwig Craven said. "Modern physics tells us that there are twenty-nine dimensions in the universe. *Our* universe, of course, only has four. Up, down; left, right; back and forth. And then, of course, time. I call our universe Four World. But there are all sorts of universes outside of Four World. We don't really know anything about them. But we do know that one of them is trying to absorb Four World."

"Absorb? What does that mean?"

Elwig Craven spread his hands. "Make it disappear."

"But—"

"Look, we don't know that much, honestly. All we know is that every time we open one of these little tunnels, something out there tries to come through and suck our universe back down through the hole."

"The people with the shadows in their eyes?"

"Whoever or whatever it is that's on the other side of that dark thing—they can't exist in this universe. They can't actually *do* anything here. But they can influence things. Weak people? People who are a little uncertain? They can kind of sneak into their brains and control them for a while. That's what's happening here."

"But . . . why is that thing—" Dale pointed at the darkness that was now looming up into the sky above them. "Why is that thing here?"

"Because of this . . . hm . . . I'm searching for the right word—*cretin*? *Moron*? *Fool*? Yes, I think *fool* would be the most accurate way of describing Mr. Robbins here. Mr. Robbins thought he could control the thing. He summoned it because he knew he could use it to control people. One of the interesting side effects of its presence here is that it causes people to forget themselves. He thought he would use that quality to control people. He would create an army of people who would do his bidding. And then he would rule the world."

Bob Robbins Jr. muttered and flopped around in the seat. He seemed completely distracted.

"As you can see, his 'clever' plan hasn't come to fruition." Elwig P. Craven looked disdainfully at Bob Robbins. "And now we're going to have to undo his handiwork."

"I still don't understand what that thing is."

"It's nothing. And it's making more nothing at an ever-increasing rate. Eventually it will turn the universe into nothing. Not the *entire* universe. Not the other dimensions. But—our world? What I call Four World? Yes, that universe will cease to exist."

"What are we going to *do*?"

"We're going to find your friend Jessica."

"She's just a kid!" Dale was starting to feel desperate now.

"Yes," said Elwig P. Craven, "she is, isn't she?"

"But . . . how can a kid save the universe?"

Elwig P. Craven looked out the window. They were whizzing past empty prairie. In the distance Dale could see the woods that surrounded the quarry. Elwig P. Craven shrugged slightly. "I haven't the faintest."

ᴑᴑᴑ

I've lost the book! Jessica thought, a feeling of horror rising inside her. She couldn't feel anything in her hand.

But then she looked over, and—to her shock—the book was right there, clutched in her blue-white fingers. What had happened was that she was so cold that she couldn't feel anything, not even the book.

Her whole body was racked with cramps now from the frigid water. It wasn't as bad up here as it was down at the bottom. But still . . . She had read a book once about the *Titanic*. It had said how long you could last in extremely cold water before hypothermia set in. It wasn't very long. She had to get out of here! Now.

She began swimming toward the side of the pond. She looked around, trying to figure out where to go. The problem was—the quarry walls rose like steep cliffs all around her. She couldn't see a way out.

Up at the top of the cliff, Cerberus was looking impassively down at her with his wolfish yellow eyes.

"Go get some help!" she called.

The dog continued to stare at her for a moment. Then it disappeared.

Jessica paddled closer to the cliffside. From the middle of the pond, it looked smooth. But now that she was closer, she could see that it was actually quite rough. There were crevices and cracks and bumps here and there.

Her first thought was that maybe she could climb out that way, more or less rock climbing the wall. But then, when she touched the wall, tried to grab hold of one of the cracks, she realized how dumb that idea was. She couldn't even feel her fingers or toes. The cliff must have been thirty or forty feet high. She probably couldn't have climbed it with climbing gear. Much less soaking wet and with frozen fingers.

Her next thought was that she was going to lose the book. If it slipped out of her hand, she'd never find it again. She saw a tiny ledge—maybe four inches wide. It looked like it might be wide enough for the book to fit on without falling off.

She reached out to set the book on the ledge. Her hand was shivering so wildly that she was afraid it might knock the book off inadvertently. But it didn't.

She took a deep breath, pulled her hand away. Would it stay?

Yes! The book lay there motionless, perched on the ledge.

Okay, she thought. *That's the first step. Now how do I get out of here before I drown?*

There had to be a way out. She just had to find it.

And then the funniest thing happened. As she started to paddle around, she felt her mind getting fuzzy. She wasn't drowning. But she just couldn't seem to concentrate. The good thing was that the cramps didn't hurt so much, and she didn't seem to be shivering so much anymore.

She paddled slowly, looking for a way out. A ladder, a rope, a set of stairs cut in the stone—anything.

And then after a while she stopped paddling. It was just too much work. And, honestly? She couldn't really remember why she'd wanted to get out anyway.

It didn't seem so cold now. Maybe her body was just getting used to it. She couldn't hold on to the side very well because her hands were so stiff.

But that was okay.

Her head went under the water. She spluttered, kicked, pulled herself up. Something in the back of her mind told her that staying under the water was not such a brilliant idea.

But once she bobbed up and took a couple more breaths, she'd could quite think what difference it would make.

Distantly she heard a dog barking.

She tried to grab hold of a crevice in the rock. But it was no good. Tired. She was so tired now. She looked around. All she could see was rock and water. The sky reflected in the water.

And something dark, something dark in the sky.

She felt a spike of terror. The dark thing. What was it? *Kick!* she thought. *Grab hold of the rock! Do something!* But her body didn't respond.

She heard a scraping sound. Her fingernails on the rock. But she couldn't feel anything at all.

She began to sink. She gulped in air. Then the water closed over her head.

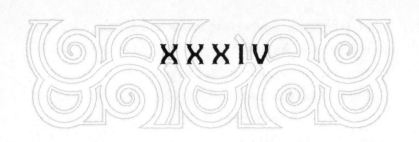

XXXIV

As the Rolls-Royce pulled up in front of the sign warning people not to trespass on the quarry property, something exploded from the bushes and flung itself against the car.

Dale's heart began to race. "Oh my God!" he said. "It's that dog!"

"That *is* quite the hound," said Elwig P. Craven III. He looked out at the huge barking dog and said, "Does anyone have a pistol?"

Bob Robbins Jr. snorted.

"What?" Elwig P. Craven said. "Is that such an absurd question?"

"That's not what I mean." Bob Robbins Jr. was huddled down in the seat with his arms folded across his chest. He looked like a teenager having a hissy fit.

"Then, pray, enlighten us," Elwig Craven said.

"It's *her* dog."

"What do you mean?"

Bob Robbins Jr. sighed loudly. "This is all a waste of

time. There's nothing we can do now. We can't outrun it, we can't stop it. It's over."

"I asked you a question, my dear fellow," Elwig Craven said. "What do you mean, 'It's her dog.'"

"Jessica. It's Jessica's dog."

"No, it's not," Dale said.

"Whatever." Bob Robbins looked out the window, stared off at the blackness that had now engulfed the entire southern horizon.

The dog was seated now, barking steadily, eyes fixed on the car. Dale's family had about half a dozen dogs, so he knew when a dog was trying to be threatening. This dog wasn't. It was more of an alert bark. Like it was trying to tell them something.

Dale felt something flash through his mind. He wasn't sure what it was. Like a memory. A memory of water. Of someone drowning.

His heart began beating hard.

"Let's go!" he shouted. Then he flung open the door and started running up the path.

Elwig Craven watched the boy disappear up the path. "Hm!" he said. "I guess we'd better go, hm?"

Bob Robbins's eyes took on a crafty gleam. "I guess," he said.

Elwig Craven climbed out of the car and started walking up the path as briskly as he could. His knees were not what they'd once been. But then, when one was over two hundred years of age, what did one expect?

After a moment Bob Robbins Jr. passed him at a slow trot. Something seemed to have gotten into him, Elwig Craven reflected.

As Dale came around the bend in the path, he found himself at the edge of the cliff, staring down at the water. The dog stood next to him, breathing heavily. It started barking down at the water.

"What's down there, boy?" Dale said.

The dog just kept barking.

And then Dale saw it. Splayed out under the water was a human figure. Long blond hair drifted around it head. *It was Jess!*

"Oh no!" he said. "What are we going to do?" *This is my fault,* he thought bitterly. *If I'd just come with her instead of being so selfish . . .*

Bob Robbins Jr. looked down into the pond. "There's the book over on that ledge," he said. "I'm getting that first."

"How?"

Bob Robbins Jr. pointed at a coil of rusting wire rope over on the far side of the quarry. Dale didn't care about the book. He just wanted to make sure Jessica was okay. As he was watching, she began slipping under the water. He immediately stripped off his shoes and jumped over the edge.

The water hit him hard, and then he was enveloped in

cold. He couldn't believe how cold it was. He fought his way toward the surface.

By the time his head cleared the water, nothing of Jessica was visible except her hair. He grabbed hold of it and started pulling. But she was too heavy. And Dale was not that great a swimmer to begin with.

"Help!" he called. "Help!"

"Forget her," Bob Robbins yelled. "Get the book."

"The book is no good without the girl," Elwig Craven said.

As Craven and Robbins began to bicker, the dog leaped off the side, hitting the water with a flat smacking sound. It swam strongly toward Dale. Dale grabbed hold of the dog, hoisting Jessica up and thrusting her limp body across the dog's back. The dog began swimming toward the side.

"The book!" Bob Robbins called. "Get the book, kid!"

Dale swam over, grabbed the book. The dog was right next to him.

"Lower the rope," he yelled. "I'll tie her on."

"You first," Bob Robbins said. "Bring the book." He was already lowering the wire rope toward them.

"The book's not coming until she's safe," Dale called back. The water was sending needles of cold through his body. But at that moment he didn't care. All he could think about was saving Jessica.

"Save yourself, kid," Bob Robbins said.

But Dale just grabbed the ragged end of the rope and

tied it around Jessica's waist. The wire rope was very stiff and didn't tie well. But it was all he had.

"Pull!" he shouted.

Bob Robbins and Elwig Craven pulled, and Jessica's limp body ascended slowly, her mouth wide open, body limp, water dripping from her blue skin.

"Hurry!" Dale called.

Slowly, slowly, slowly she ascended.

"Now the book."

"What about the dog?" Dale said.

"Forget that freaky thing," Bob Robbins yelled.

Dale shook his head. "It saved both of our lives," Dale said. "The dog goes up next."

"You're a moron, you know that," Bob Robbins called back.

Dale waited for the rope, tied it onto the dog.

Bob Robbins and Elwig Craven heaved on the rope. But the dog didn't move.

"It's too heavy," Bob Robbins called. "It's got to be you."

"But—"

"He's right, Dale," Elwig Craven called. "The animal will have to fend for itself."

"But—"

"There's no time for debate." Elwig Craven's voice cracked out like a whip. "Do it!"

Dale obediently untied the dog and looped the rope around his own hips. "Okay," he called.

As soon as he had cleared the lip of the hill, Elwig Craven dropped to his knees and put his head on Jessica's chest. "Still beating," he said. "Not strongly, though." He turned her head to the side.

Dale felt sick with worry. Jessica wasn't moving at all. *All my fault!* he thought again. *All my fault!*

"How are your lifesaving skills, Mr. Robbins?" Elwig Craven said.

"Do I look like the lifeguard type?" Bob Robbins Jr. said.

Elwig Craven narrowed his eyes for a moment. "Point taken," he said. He turned Jessica's head and pressed hard on her chest. She spit up what seemed like about a gallon of water and then started choking loudly.

Dale jumped on top of her and hugged her. Her skin felt cold as a refrigerator. "Jessica!" he shouted. "Jessica! You're okay!"

"Gimme the book," Bob Robbins Jr. said. The vacuum cleaner salesman grabbed Dale, spun him around, and attempted to yank the book out of his hand.

"Let go of it," Elwig Craven said.

But by then Bob Robbins had the book in his hand. "Or what?" he said, his eyes glinting.

"Or . . . this," Elwig Craven said, pulling the gold head off his cane. As he did so, the thin man revealed a curiously designed pistol.

Bob Robbins Jr. glared at him. "You said you didn't have a—"

"I lied," Elwig Craven said. "One of my favorite things about words is that they don't have to tell the truth all the time. Now drop it."

Bob Robbins made a face of disgust. But he dropped the book.

"Let's get the girl to the car," Elwig Craven said.

Dale looked down into the water. The dog was swimming uncomplainingly in a circle.

"What about—"

"There's no time," Elwig Craven said, pointing to the south. The dark thing had blotted out almost half the horizon now, rising high into the sky like some kind of infernal thunderstorm. "We have to go."

XXXV

Jessica was deep inside the dark thing. She didn't feel cold, didn't feel anything at all. Just empty blackness. No up, no down. And yet somehow she felt like there was someplace she needed to go. And then she heard someone calling her name. A distant voice. Someone she knew.

"Jessica! Jessica!"

Dale. It was Dale.

She swam toward his voice, swam with all her might.

"Jessica!"

And then suddenly the darkness seemed to clear. And she found herself lying on the seat of a car. A large car.

"Jessica!"

She turned. And there was Dale, soaking wet and shivering, his eyes focused deeply on hers. "Jessica?"

She felt a weak smile spreading across her face. She choked a little, then sat up. "Hey," she said. "What's going on?"

"You found the book!" Dale said.

The book. She scratched her head. She realized that she was wet and shivering, too. The book. The book. She had no idea what he was talking about.

"*Her Lif*! The book! You found it!"

Two men were sitting across from her. A thin dapper man in an old-fashioned tailcoat and another guy who looked like somebody had just taken his ice-cream cone away. She associated him with vacuum cleaners. Though she couldn't really remember why.

"What's a *lif*?" she said.

"A what?"

"Her *lif*," Jessica said. "You just said, 'her *lif*.' That's not even a word."

Dale looked at the two men across from them and said, "Um. This is not good."

Back at the quarry, the dog continued to circle the pond. His swimming had been strong and sure at first. But now he began to whimper a little. And sometimes his head slipped under the water for a second or two.

After a moment a tall blond woman walked out of the trees. In her hand was a white cane.

"Cerberus?" she called.

The dog whimpered.

"Cerberus," she called. "I'm with you."

The dog barked once, loudly. Then, after a few more strokes, its head sank beneath the water.

The blind woman at the top of the cliff aimed her face down toward the water. Then she took off her sunglasses. Her sightless eyes began to stream with tears.

"Give her the book, Dale," the thin man in the old-fashioned clothes said.

Dale handed Jessica a soggy old book. Its pages were all puffed up and ripply. She opened it. You could still read the book okay, though.

As she leafed through it, things began to come back to her. Elwig Craven. Bob Robbins Jr.

And then she felt it. The dark thing. Her mouth tasted horrible, and her stomach felt sick.

The dark thing had been inside of her.

"Oh, God!" she said. Then she looked out the window, knowing it would be out there. To the left of the car all she could see was endless prairie and a clear blue sky. But in front of them was a boiling darkness. And it was coming toward them—faster and faster and faster.

"All right, stop the car, Floyd," Elwig Craven said to the driver.

The driver stopped. They all got out. They had reached the edge of the huge crowd. No one was walking toward the dark thing anymore. They were just milling around now. No shadows flickered in their eyes. They just seemed blank now, like empty people.

The great roiling blackness rose above them like a wall.

It seemed to have split the earth in half. On this side—the world. On that side—nothingness.

The air was cold, and the light seemed pale and weak. All the colors around them had faded into shades of gray.

"Why are we here?" Bob Robbins said loudly. "There's nothing she can do now. It's too strong."

Jessica could barely hear him. It was as though the dark thing was sucking everything into it now. Sound, light, heat—everything. It felt as though the great dark thing was coming to a boil, just about to explode or something.

And then everything stopped.

The black thing ceased to move. The crowd turned and stared blankly at it. No one spoke. No one moved. For what must have been several minutes, it seemed as though the earth itself had ceased to turn.

"What's it doing?" Dale said.

Elwig Craven shouted back, "It's about to happen." Elwig Craven looked like he was shouting. But his voice was like a whisper coming from the end of a long, long tunnel.

"*What's* about to happen?"

Elwig Craven didn't speak.

"What's it going to *do*?" Dale shouted in his tiny, distant voice.

And then, without warning, Jessica knew. The answer was just *there*. "Tertiary phase," she said.

"What?" Dale shouted.

"Tertiary phase."

"What does that mean?" The veins were popping up on Dale's neck as he struggled to make himself heard. The silence was intensifying.

Suddenly the wind began to gather. Blowing straight toward the darkness. It blew faster and faster.

The air was full of grass and dust. The people in the crowd crouched down and covered their heads. There was no sound, though. No whistling, no roar—just the feeling of pressure, pushing them, pushing them—as though it would lift them all off their feet and hurl them into the darkness.

"Hold on!" Jessica shouted. But her voice made no sound at all.

Bits of grass and dirt stung her face.

"Down!" she yelled.

But she didn't need to say anything. Everybody was hunkering down, covering their heads.

The wind blew faster and faster. Jessica tried to find cover behind the Rolls-Royce. But Bob Robbins shoved her out of the way, then lay down, covering his head. His mouth was open in a noiseless scream.

And then, as quickly as it had started, it was gone.

For a moment no one moved. Finally Bob Robbins Jr. sat up timidly, looked around. "Holy mackerel!" he said. "It's gone!"

He turned and pointed.

And it was true. The blackness had utterly disappeared.

Suddenly people in the crowd started talking. There was a buzz of conversation. People were looking around, puzzled.

"You did it, Jessica!" Dale shouted. "You *did* it!"

Jessica looked at him sadly, then she shook her head.

She remembered everything now. "Follow me," she said sadly.

"What?" Dale said.

She stood and started walking through the crowd, holding the soggy book in front of her. Elwig Craven and Bob Robbins Jr. followed. They didn't have to walk far. Jessica found what she was looking for about a hundred yards away.

It was a vacuum. The Pow-R-Kleen 5000.

"Hey!" Bob Robbins Jr. said. "That's mine. Give me that!"

"Don't touch it," she said.

"Why not?"

"The dark thing," Jessica said. "It's not gone."

She pointed at the ground. Next to the Pow-R-Kleen 5000 was a small bright spot, so bright you couldn't look at it. It was like looking at an arc welder.

"What is it?" Bob Robbins Jr. said.

"You want to tell him, Mr. Craven?" she said. She was feeling so sad now that she could barely talk.

"Tertiary phase," Elwig Craven said. "Those dark things have four stages. Primary stage, it's a little ball of darkness. It grows slowly. But otherwise it does nothing. Secondary phase, it starts heaving and boiling and all those tendrils come out and snatch things. It gets bigger and bigger and more and more furious. And then, suddenly, it implodes. That's what just happened."

Bob Robbins Jr. looked down at the bright spot, shielding his eyes. "Huh," he said. "Didn't know that."

"You should have done a little more research, young man," Elwig Craven said.

Bob Robbins stared apprehensively at the bright speck. "Tertiary phase, huh."

"Didn't you say it has a fourth phase, Jess?" Dale said.

She nodded.

"What happens then?" Dale pursued.

Just as she was about to answer, she heard a voice call to her. "Jess! There you are! Oh my gosh, we were worried sick about you!"

She turned and saw her mother racing toward her through the crowd. Her father was right behind her, his face split by a huge grin. It was her *real* mother, too. Not the sad creature she'd seen living over on Rose Lane. Her mother grabbed her and hugged her. Her father threw his arms around both of them.

"Oh, honey," he said, "you gave us a heck of a scare!" It was her real dad, the one who was shift foreman at the sausage factory, the one who read *Pork Processing Monthly* and laughed all the time. Not the crippled guy who sat out back listening to the Twins and throwing an old tennis ball against the side of the shed.

She felt their arms around her, and she started to cry.

"I know, I know," her mother said softly.

Jessica finally pushed her mother and father away. "No," she said. "You don't know."

They looked at her, puzzled. Then her father turned and pointed at the bright speck on the ground. "What's that, hon?"

"It's a tertiary phase chronoplastic singularity," she said.

Everyone in the group looked at her, waiting for a further explanation.

"You know the Big Bang?" she said to Dale.

"Yeah," he said. "That's how the universe started. Everything in the whole universe went exploding out of this tiny little speck of—"

His eyes widened.

"Wait a minute!" Bob Robbins Jr. said. "Are you saying—"

"The universe was formed out of a quaternary phase chronoplastic singularity." She paused. "This is a tertiary phase. That means it's in the third phase right now. When it reaches the fourth . . . Well, let's put it this way: when that thing blows up, our entire universe disappears."

There was a brief silence.

"Well, uh . . . ," Bob Robbins Jr. said. "When's that gonna happen?"

"It's impossible to predict," Jessica said. She wasn't sure how she knew this stuff. But she knew. No question, she totally knew. She remembered. "It could happen in a minute, a day . . . maybe a thousand years from now."

"Oh." Bob Robbins stroked his face. "Well, you know what then? Then I'm not gonna worry about it."

"Yeah," Jessica said. "But the thing is, it's not supposed to happen. The universe is supposed to keep going. Just like it has been."

Bob Robbins Jr. chuckled. "Not my problem, sweetie pie. Not my problem."

"Don't you talk to my daughter like that, young man!" Jessica's dad said.

Jessica smiled fondly at her father. He was such a sweet man. A little dull. But sweet.

"Mom," she said. "Dad. Could you go stand over there for a minute?" She pointed at the Rolls-Royce.

"Why?" her mother said.

"I just have to wrap some stuff up with these guys."

Her mother and father exchanged glances, then gave her a hug and walked off toward the limousine. Jessica looked around at all the people in the crowd. They were talking pleasantly, walking around, kids playing tag, young couples holding hands. Nobody seemed to be wondering why they were all standing in the middle of the empty prairie.

"So, this is it," Elwig Craven said sadly to her.

"You knew?"

He nodded. "Go ahead," he said. "Read."

She opened the soggy book. Sandwiched between the cover and the first page was a small piece of paper. At the top it read:

❖ *Erratum* ❖

On page 631, the sentence ending, ". . . and she returned to her happy, normal life" is in error.

The correct passage should be—

She didn't read what the correct passage should be, though. There was something about it that made her feel apprehensive and nervous. She closed the book.

"I can't," she said in a small voice.

"Dale," Elwig Craven said. "Would you help her out?"

Jessica handed the book to Dale. "Read the erratum page," she said.

Dale opened the book and began reading: "'On page 631, the sentence ending, ". . . and she returned to her happy, normal life" is in error. The correct passage is as follows.'" He looked up. "The whole thing? It's like a pretty long page."

Jessica felt sadder than she had ever felt before. The blind woman at the library had been right. She was in for a lot of sadness. She remembered it all now. Why couldn't everything have just stayed the same? Why did she have to find this stupid book anyway? It just wasn't fair. She looked over at her parents. They were standing by the car, chatting away, no idea of what was going on.

"Go ahead, Dale," she said softly.

Dale read again. "The correct passage is as follows. 'Jessica continued to live in the smallest, cheapest, dirtiest house on the poorest street of Alsberg, Minnesota. As the years went by, her father's health continued to deteriorate. He grew more bitter and more angry by the day. Her mother, faced with the pressure of poverty and unhappiness, was unable to—'"

Dale broke off. Tears started pouring down his face. "No!" he said. "No, no, no! That's not *right!*"

Jessica nodded. "All this time?" she said. "All this time, you know, I always used to say how I felt like I was in the wrong family, the wrong place?"

"No . . ." Dale said softly.

"Well, it was true. We both were."

"That nice guy that you always dreamed of playing touch football with? That nice mom who baked cookies every day and checked your homework and bought books for you?"

"No . . ."

"That *is* your real family."

"But what about you?"

Jessica didn't answer.

"She has a choice," Elwig Craven said. "She has a choice."

"What choice?" Bob Robbins Jr. said.

"There's only one person who can switch this thing

off," Elwig Craven said, pointing at the Pow-R-Kleen 5000. "There's only one person who can restore the universe to the way it's supposed to be. See, if she chooses, she can go back to those nice folks over there." He pointed at her mother and father. "They love her very much. They'll always say, 'There's something *different* about Jessica.' But they'll be proud of it. Proud of her. Proud of her lif."

"Her *life* you mean?" Dale said.

Elwig Craven smiled sadly. "No. Her lif. Because it won't be *her* life. It'll be something else. A mistake. An error. A flaw in the universe."

"I don't get this," Bob Robbins Jr. said. "This is giving me a headache."

Elwig Craven gave him a hard look.

"You said she had a choice . . ." Bob Robbins said.

"It's right there," Elwig Craven said. "She can make the tertiary phase chronoplastic singularity go away. Or not. If she lets it stay here—then we all stay right here." He waved his arm around them.

And somehow, without anybody quite noticing it, Alsberg, Minnesota, had come back. Not exactly the same. But almost. The sausage factory was in a slightly different place. The library, too. But it was all there. Every house, every tree, every store, every person.

They were standing about twenty feet from the front door of the library.

"If she stays here," Elwig Craven said, "so will the singularity. And one day—maybe tomorrow, maybe a thousand years from now—the entire universe will be destroyed." He took a long, slow breath, then sighed sadly. "On the other hand, if she decides to get rid of it, we'll all go back to where we're supposed to be. The error in the universe will be repaired. But when that happens . . ." Elwig Craven pointed at her parents. They were standing by the curb now, next to the new Pontiac her dad had just bought. The couple smiled and waved. "Those nice people will disappear from the universe forever."

Jessica felt tears running down her face.

"There is a compensation, though," Elwig Craven said softly to her. "You'll become Jessica Sternhagen. *The* Jessica Sternhagen. The girl who saved the universe."

"So, sweetie," Bob Robbins Jr. said. "What's it gonna be?"

"Let me see the book," she said. "I still haven't found out exactly what it is I'm supposed to do. I mean, I must have to actually *do* something to make it go away. Right?"

She took the book back from Dale, flipped it open, started reading. It was a description of a school field trip in sixth grade. She flipped a few more chapters. The ink was a little faded, but she could still read it. The science fair where she got first prize for growing praying mantises. She flipped another twenty pages. With a sinking feeling, she noticed that the ink was getting paler and paler. It was harder and harder to read.

"Oh no," she said.

"What?" Dale said.

She started turning pages as quickly as the soggy paper

would allow. As she got closer and closer to the present, the words began fading into nothingness. Soon, they were like ghosts. She was supposed to remember something, right? But how? The letters were literally disappearing on the page.

"I don't remember," she said desperately. "I don't remember."

"Remember what?" Dale said.

She got to the last few pages. There was simply nothing there. No instructions. No memories. No recipes or formulas. Nothing at all. Just empty pages.

Jessica suddenly felt a sense of betrayal. It had all been some kind of big joke. From the very beginning, there had been no hope, no answers here. It was all just a big tease. *Hey, kid—wanna save the universe?* Yeah, right! What a joke. A lame, stupid, mean joke.

She handed the book back to Dale.

"Give me a minute," Jessica said.

Then she walked away from Dale and the two men. It only took her a few seconds to reach her parents. But in her mind it seemed to take a long time. When she reached them, Jessica gave her mother and father each a big hug.

"What's *that* for?" her mother said, with a puzzled smile.

Jessica shrugged. "I just felt like it."

Her mother and father looked at each other and gave each other a fond smile.

"She *is* different," her mother said, still with the same fond smile.

"Yes, she is," her father said, putting his arm around her neck and giving her a squeeze. "And we like her that way."

"Ready to go, hon?" her mother said.

Jessica stood stock-still. All she had to do was get in the car. And she could keep this. She could keep it *all*. Maybe the universe would end tomorrow. But in the meantime, she would have this. All this happiness.

Jessica took a deep breath, smiled, and climbed in the backseat of the Pontiac. "Let's go home," she said.

XXXVI

"**S**o much for the big hero," Bob Robbins Jr. said as the shiny red Pontiac drove down the street.

"Huh," Dale said. "I guess I never really knew her at all." He watched the Pontiac drive off down the street. He could see the back of her head in the window. She never looked back. Then the car disappeared around the corner.

Dale turned to Elwig Craven and added, "But still, I feel kinda good for her, you know?"

"Even though she just decided to let the universe blow up?" Bob Robbins Jr. said sharply.

"Hey, it's only Four World," Dale said. "There's still like twenty-five more dimensions out there, right?"

"That's very philosophical of you," Bob Robbins Jr. said.

"So what happens now?" Dale said to Elwig Craven.

Before Elwig Craven could answer, though, the shiny red Pontiac came back up the street and parked. Jessica climbed out and ran back across the courtyard.

"I just remembered!" she called to them.

"Remembered what?"

"The book," she called, still running toward them. "I forgot my book."

Dale realized he'd been holding on to it so hard that his fingers were hurting. He extended it toward her.

As she came to a halt, their eyes met for a moment.

"You know what this means, don't you?" Elwig Craven said softly.

"Yes," Jessica said firmly. "I know."

They all stood there silently, eyes focused on the book, *Her Lif*. Finally she reached out and took the book.

For a moment nothing happened. But then, slowly, slowly, the tiny brilliant light on the ground next to the vacuum cleaner faded away. And after a few seconds, it winked out entirely.

Dale was a little surprised. He had expected something showy. Flashing lights, big machines, magic wands, explosions, creepy noises . . . *something*. A big show. But, no. Whatever she'd done to turn the singularity off—whatever switch she'd thrown—it was all inside her head.

"I'll be dadgum!" Bob Robbins Jr. said. "She just saved the universe!"

"Of course she did," Elwig Craven said with a smile. "She's Jessica Sternhagen."

XXXVII

For a moment—just a moment—Jessica remembered everything. The dark thing was an error, an erratum in the universe. It needed to be fixed, edited, expurgated, written out of the story. She remembered how it was supposed to be, what was supposed to happen, how the book was supposed to end. And in that moment she knew she had the choice—to remember . . . or to forget. If she remembered the way the story was *supposed* to end, the way the universe was *supposed* to be, then the erratum would be corrected. And the dark thing would unhappen.

But it wasn't that simple. Everything was connected. You couldn't unhappen one thing without unhappening a lot of other stuff. Bob Robbins had stolen the machine that summoned the dark thing a very long time ago. A lot of things had happened since he took it from Victor the Moldavian. To unhappen the dark thing, a lot of other events would have to unhappen, too.

The happy life she'd been living all these years? The nice house, the church picnics, the trips to the beach, the pleasant Mom and Dad, the happy family—it all had to go.

If she wanted to stop the dark thing, she had to remember the other, truer, sadder life. She had to choose it, make that life her own.

But what could she do? It was her destiny.

She smiled. You took the good with the bad, didn't you? And this wasn't *so* bad. After all, how many people got to say that it was their destiny to save the world? That was kind of cool, you had to admit.

As Dale handed Jessica the book he'd been holding for her, a thin dapper man wearing an old-fashioned tuxedo picked up a vacuum cleaner that had been sitting on the granite courtyard next to them, and threw it over his shoulder.

"Hey, wait a minute!" a second man said. He was younger, casually dressed, with lots of hair gel. "That's mine!"

"Not anymore," the dapper man said. "You can't be trusted with it."

"It's *mine!*"

"Don't you understand, Bob? They used you. The dark things used you. They wanted you to open up that singularity so they could suck our universe off into oblivion. And you're so dumb, you played right into their hands."

"Now listen here—"

The two men walked away arguing. Dale and Jessica watched them approach a long Rolls-Royce that was parked at the curb. The younger man tried to grab the vacuum. But then a very large man in a chauffeur's uniform jumped out, and the younger man backed up nervously. The chauffeur took the vacuum and put it in the trunk of the limo. Then he and the dapper man got in the limousine and drove away.

The younger guy yelled something after them, shook his fist, then climbed into a van that said POW-R-KLEEN INDUSTRIES on the side. He revved his engine and skidded away from the curb, tires smoking, heading off in the opposite direction.

"What are you smiling about?" Dale said to Jessica.

"Nothing special," she said. "I'm just in a good mood, I guess." Jessica felt her smile fade. For a moment she had felt the strongest sense of accomplishment and fulfillment. And yet she couldn't for the life of her think why she was feeling that way. She hadn't done anything in particular today. Not that she could remember anyway.

Dale looked at his watch. "Well, I guess I better get home," he said. "Dad said he was gonna play touch football with us in the yard as soon as he gets off work. You wanna come?"

Jessica shrugged. Sometimes she liked being at Dale's, sometimes not. There were times when being around all the cheeriness in his family just made her depressed, made her think of her sullen mother, made her think of her father, sitting out behind the house, the scar on his forehead, the monotonous *thump thump thump* of his tennis ball against the wall of the garage.

"Come on, Jess! It'll be fun. Dad's grilling Polish sausages tonight."

Jessica sighed. For some reason she just felt like being alone. "Nah. I think I'll go to the library. This book is due today. Mom screamed at me for like an hour last time I had to pay a fine."

Dale reached out and turned the book around so he could read the cover. "*Her Life.* Huh. Any good?"

Jessica frowned. She had the weirdest feeling for a minute, like she was supposed to know what the book was about. But she was darned if she could remember.

"I don't know," she said. "I never got around to reading it."

EPILOGUE

The tiny man lay motionless at the bottom of the pool. After a while his lips moved. Almost as though he was speaking. But of course underwater it was impossible to hear him. A bubble rose from his lips and went wobbling up through the water.

When it hit the surface of the water, it burst with a tiny, moist pop.

If anyone had been there to hear it—and had listened very hard—they would have heard Alphonse B. Margarine's voice issuing forth from the bubble. A tiny, tiny ghostly echo of a voice. A voice speaking one single word.

"Bluntwiiiiiick!"

But there was, in fact, no one there to hear it.

Unless you counted the huge dog that stood at the top of the rock cliff, looking down at the water with its strange yellow eyes.

But, after all, that's another story.